I0615558

John Frederick Smith

Frederick Swanwick

A sketch

John Frederick Smith

Frederick Swanwick
A sketch

ISBN/EAN: 9783337012908

Printed in Europe, USA, Canada, Australia, Japan

Cover: Foto ©Raphael Reischuk / pixelio.de

More available books at **www.hansebooks.com**

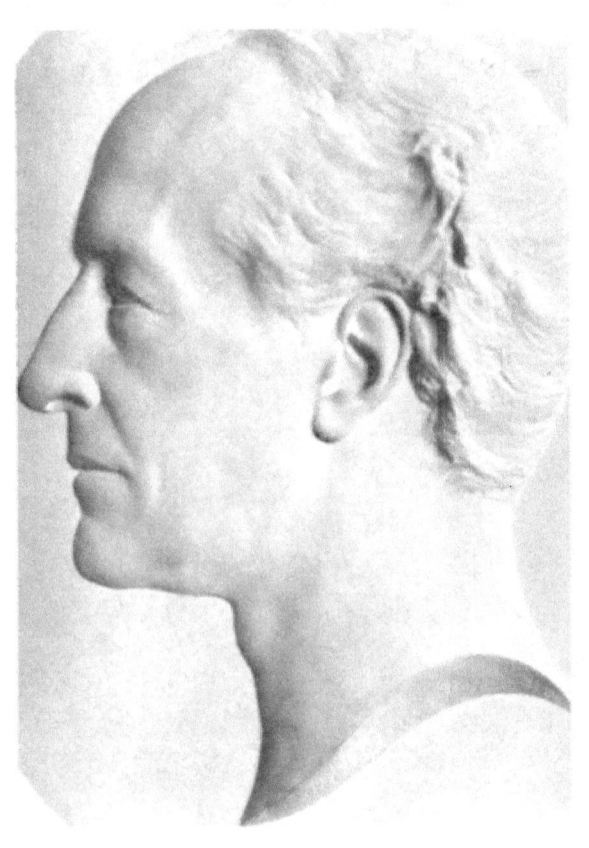

FREDERICK SWANWICK

A Sketch

BY

J. FREDERICK SMITH

"QUEM NEMO NON PARUM AMAT, ETIAM QUI AMARE PLUS NON POTEST"

Seneca

PRINTED FOR PRIVATE CIRCULATION

1888

CONTENTS.

PREFACE.

It was my good fortune to make the acquaintance of Mr. Frederick Swanwick in the spring of 1870. The acquaintance soon grew into a cordial friendship for the remainder of his life. For eleven years it was my privilege to be much in his society, and to work with him, or to enjoy the advantage of his support, in various religious, educational, political, and social activities. In describing his character I have done nothing more than speak of him as I found him in every relation of life. The debt of gratitude I owe to him is great and varied, and such that it can never be discharged. But it is a deep satisfaction to me to be permitted, encouraged, and helped by his family to draw up this slight sketch of his life and character, as some expression of a keen sense of the debt as well as of great love and respect for a friend never to be forgotten by me or mine. Most sincerely do I wish that one more able to execute worthily the task had come forward to trace for his friends the story of his life and the beauty of his character. But as, in default of such a one, the duty might be neglected, I believe the love of a large circle of friends for their friend is so strong that it will avail to excuse the weaknesses of my pen and to procure thanks to his family for sanctioning an imperfect, rather than no written memorial of a life of such rare excellence.

It is a great satisfaction to me to be able, by the kind permission of the writer, to place here a letter written in reply to a request for recollections of Mr. Swanwick's life or impressions of his character. The Rev. Thomas Hincks, closely connected with Mr. Swanwick by family ties, and for many years a very dear and intimate friend of his, appeared to me better qualified than any one else to render the help so much needed. The reader of his letter will be thankful for the loving, delicate, and faithful characterization which, as a picture in miniature, it gives of our dear friend :—

LEIGH WOODS, BRISTOL,
October 1886.

DEAR MR. SMITH,—You will not, I am sure, ascribe my delay in replying to your letter to any unwillingness to comply with your request, or to indifference as to the work which you have undertaken. I am truly glad that you, who knew Frederick Swanwick so well, and appreciated him so fully, are to give us a sketch of his life and character. If I could help you in any measure, I would most willingly do so. But, on thinking the matter over, I hardly see what I could contribute that would be of any positive value to you.

The little that I knew of our friend's early career I gathered from conversations into which I almost *forced* him, so reticent was he, as you know, about himself. I learned from them how early and completely he won the confidence of Stephenson, the heavy responsibilities which were cast upon him by his chief, and the energy and resource with which he fulfilled them. But of all this you will no doubt obtain more precise accounts from other sources.

As to his character, it was so winning, so transparent, so readable by all who had the great privilege of knowing him, that I do not think my intimacy with him, close as it was, would enable me to tell much more of it than it told of itself.

Some of his characteristics (at least in the degree in which he manifested them) seem to me, as I look back over my life, unique in my experience. There was a *radiancy* about him, an overflowing geniality, telling so plainly of a finely-tempered heart, which were irresistible and contagious, and which made his presence like a perpetual sunshine. No one could be insensible to the graciousness, and delicacy, and pure self-forgetfulness which he manifested in his social relations. It was a curious study (if one were ever in a mood to treat such a matter critically) to watch how he would contrive the most delicate kindnesses for his friends, making them feel all the while as if he were the obliged party, and they were the benefactors. His genial qualities made him the perfection of a host, and it was one of the choice experiences of life to be a guest in his house; yet it was not mere geniality that rendered him so attractive to all who were brought into relation with him; he was as bright and animated intellectually as he was courteous and considerate and sympathetic to all.

And then with all the quick intelligence, the fine intellectual gifts and culture, which, as you know, he possessed, he was simple as the child, without a trace, that I could ever detect, of assumption or pretence, always eager to learn from those who had anything to teach him, and ever ready to place himself in sympathy, if it were possible, with others, though their tastes and pursuits might be different from his own.

You know well (to pass from the sphere of his home life) what a power for good he was as a citizen. You had opportunities of judging of this which I had not. But no one could know Mr. Swanwick without recognising in him a true philanthropist, indifferent to nothing which might promote the elevation of the people. He was by no means a dilettante philanthropist, but an earnest, thoughtful worker for the objects he had at heart. He spent himself, and he spent his money, freely and wisely in the service of others. Education was probably the subject which interested him most deeply; on this he had read and thought much, and held very definite and decided opinions, to which he never lost an opportunity of giving practical effect. He was a sturdy opponent of the old scholastic system, and always ready to run a tilt at the "dead languages!" It was delightful to witness (as I have done in many a keen but friendly encounter at his house) the vigour and enthusiasm with which he would attack the absurdities of the classical system, and plead for a broader and more catholic conception of the educational work. But apart from all his special labours for the general good, the value of his personal character to the public life of his neighbourhood must, as it seems to me, have been immense. It inspired absolute trust, and it *won the heart* at the same time. One point more, and I have done.

He was a man who had a large acquaintance with the world and its ways, and had been long and variously engaged in its work, yet he never lost through mature and advanced life the lightheartedness, the guilelessness, and the fresh enthusiasm which are commonly associated with youth. To the last he was never anything but youthful in heart.

It was a high privilege to know him, and for myself I feel that life was distinctly impoverished by his removal. His memory should not be lost, and I rejoice that you are to do what is possible to perpetuate it.

His fine head and bright speaking countenance, which was never a mask, but rather, as it were, a window through which his heart was always looking out, will remain amongst the pleasantest of memories to those who knew him well, and loved him as those who knew him well were bound to do.

I fear that these few personal impressions of our friend's character will be of little service to you. But at any rate they will show you how he appeared to one who had many opportunities of learning what he really was.—— Believe me, with very kind remembrances, very sincerely yours, THOMAS HINCKS.

Rev. J. F. SMITH.

The readers of this sketch are indebted to Mr. Arnold Lupton for an interesting Note amongst the Appendixes, on some of the distinguishing aspects of Mr. Swanwick's work as an engineer, with a tabular statement of the principal railways on which he was engaged.

It is greatly to be regretted that the materials for an adequate sketch of Mr. Swanwick's life do not exist. His friends will also lament that no portrait doing anything like justice to his fine countenance was ever taken. But they will be glad to have the two photographs which are here given. The full-length photograph was taken some time between 1861 and 1864, and is less unsatisfactory than any subsequent one. The medallion, of which a photograph is given, was sculptured by Mr. Albert Bruce Joy from that and other photographs with the aid of a cast taken after death.

J. FREDERICK SMITH.

FREDERICK SWANWICK.

—◆—

FREDERICK SWANWICK was born October 1, 1810, in the quaint, historic city of Chester, whose walls, arcades, bridges, river and surrounding scenery, remained dear to him through life. He was the youngest of four brothers, and had but one sister, younger than himself, who alone survives him. His father, Joseph Swanwick, was descended from Philip Henry, the well-known ejected minister. Joseph Swanwick, together with his brothers, received the earlier part of his education at Wem, from Hazlitt, the father of the author and of the painter. He afterwards, with a view to the Dissenting Ministry, went to the Dissenting Academy at Hackney, in the conduct of which Dr. Priestley had succeeded to Dr. Price, and the Doctor's lectures made a lasting impression on him. But he finally gave up his intention of entering the ministry, and devoted himself to business in Chester. He must have been a man of much more than ordinary intelligence and cultivation, and of very decided political ability. He took a keen and active interest in the commercial and political affairs of his country generally, and of Chester in particular. Speeches of his,

A

which have been preserved in an interesting pamphlet,[1] show that he was not only a most earnest, fearless, and enlightened politician, but also a speaker of very marked ability and popular power. Letters which have been preserved, addressed to him by his bosom friend Mr. John Wicksteed of Shrewsbury, supply evidence of the wide range of his reading, and of the ardour of his political sympathies. Frederick was often an eager listener to the conversations on social and political topics which his father and like-minded men of the city were in the habit of holding, and thus early the boy's interest in such matters may have been formed. A niece of Mr. Joseph Swanwick's supplies the following reminiscences of her uncle :—

" With regard to my dear uncle, my own recollections of him are that he was considered a man of great intellectual vigour, a very keen politician, in fact, the Liberal leader of Chester. He was a born political orator, and his townsmen fully appreciated this gift. I have heard it said, or rather mourned over, that his office was always full of politicians, which, of course, sadly interfered with business. He was, however, not formed for business, having been educated at Hackney Academy, the Unitarian College of those days, and intended for the ministry. But in the course of his studies he changed his religious opinions, and on that account did not seek to take a pulpit. He was loving, affectionate, and full of fun, so that he was a great favourite with us all. I remember being told that at one time

---

[1] *A Narration of the Memorable Contest for the Representation of Chester in 1826. Chester 1826.*

when there was some political agitation going on, a large deputation waited upon him, and insisted on seeing him, though he was only just recovering from an illness and had not left his room, and that no entreaties of my aunt could prevent his dressing and going down to speak to them."

Frederick's mother, *née* Hannah Wicksteed, was a woman of great energy and strength of character, with a strong love of poetry and fine music. The same niece gives the following description of her:—

" My aunt was a woman of great simplicity of character, full of life and energy, impulsive and enthusiastic, kind-hearted and affectionate. She had a vivid imagination which enabled her to delight in the best poets, and made her an ardent admirer of nature. Her love of scenery was quite remarkable, and was inherited, I think, in an equal degree by her son Frederick. She was a constant reader of the Unitarian periodicals of the day, and all but worshipped Dr. Channing. How we all loved her! I must not omit the fact that she was an excellent housewife."

Frederick's first school was that of his maiden aunts, Mary and Martha Wicksteed, two highly cultivated women, for whom he ever after entertained great respect and affection. Reminiscences of his sister's, Mrs. Thomas Swanwick, jotted down in 1840, from these early years, recall the bright chubby boy, with a rosy face full of thought and sunshine, but withal self-possessed and determined, without fear of any man. Thoughtfulness, radiancy, independence, and courage remained striking features of the man as of the boy.

Summer sojourns in rural quarters in Flintshire during the holidays remained through life bright spots in Mr. Swanwick's memory of his boyish days. The children enjoyed in these retreats the freedom of the country, and the excitement, to them so great, of visits to the farms near at hand, and to the seashore, to which was added the crowning delight of hearing a novel of Sir Walter Scott's read aloud to them by their mother. Visits, in these early years, to his aunts in Ireland, and the companionship there of many of his cousins, also left lasting impressions on Frederick's mind.

From the school of his aunts, Frederick passed into that of the Rev. William Bakewell, the Unitarian minister at Chester, of whose congregation his parents and aunts were members. Here it was that his bright intelligence, when he was about twelve or thirteen years of age, attracted the attention of the Rev. Dr. Hutton, who was then minister of the Mill Hill Chapel, Leeds, and related to the Swanwicks by a common descent from Philip Henry. Like many of the Presbyterian and Unitarian ministers of that time, Dr. Hutton added to the duties of a preacher and pastor those of a schoolmaster. Struck by the evident signs of intelligence and strength of character in the lad, Dr. Hutton asked his parents to let him take him back with him to Leeds, urging the argument that the presence of such a boy in his school would be the means of keeping up its tone. The offer was willingly accepted by Mr. Swanwick, who had a large family to educate on very limited means, and valued highly the character and attainments of Dr.

Hutton. Frederick remained in the Doctor's school some two or three years, and contracted an esteem and affectionate regard for his master, which continued unabated to the last. His bright face always grew brighter whenever in after-life the name of Dr. Hutton was mentioned. Mr. John Hutton, son of Dr. Hutton, states that Mr. Swanwick attributed to the training he received under his father his habit of thinking earnestly and "below the surface."[1] In conversation, when Dr. Hutton was referred to, Mr. Swanwick would speak with admiration of the deep feeling, polished style, and exquisite imagery of his sermons. The curriculum of the school seems to have consisted of Latin, Greek, French, and some elementary mathematics, but of course did not in those days include "science." In after-life Mr. Swanwick looked back with keen regret upon the time which he, in common with all schoolboys of his day, spent on Latin and Greek, to the entire neglect of scientific subjects. To English composition, however, attention was given. Fragments of Frederick's "corrected compositions" have happily escaped the destruction which has so ruthlessly attended all other autograph traces of his boyhood. They are dated August 30th and September 5th, 1824, and supply not only evidence of the moral tone of Dr. Hutton's tuition, and of the pains bestowed on the writing of good English, but are also singularly prophetic of the principles and habits of his pupil's subsequent life. The motto of the first of them is, "Whatsoever thy hand findeth to do, do

---

[1] *In Memoriam. Frederick Swanwick, M.I.C.E.* 1886. Printed also in *Proceedings of the Institution of Civil Engineers*, Session 1885-86, Part iii.

it with thy might." We who knew the man at home or
abroad, at work or at play, on the magisterial bench or in
committees, as a philanthropist or a politician, can hardly
help being startled that the boy of fourteen should have
selected this motto, of which his entire subsequent life was
to be an exposition and illustration of really wonderful force
and completeness. The second topic is " Order ; " the third,
" To neglect money in the proper season is sometimes the
greatest gain ; " the fourth, " Studies nourish youth and
delight old age." These also are remarkably characteristic,
and present the boy as " father of the man."

Though Frederick was not, like his elder brothers, sent
to a public school, and did not after leaving Dr. Hutton's
pursue further the study of the ancient languages, his
attainments in them were probably quite as advanced at
the age of sixteen as those of industrious and clever boys
at that point usually are. The amount of attention he had
given at school to Latin and Greek was enough to fully
qualify him to form in after years an opinion as to the
value of a classical training in the case of boys who are
destined to pursue in future life special lines of study of
which Latin and Greek form no part.

One or two recollections of Frederick as a schoolboy
have been preserved. An old and dear friend of his, who
was spared to survive him, Miss Hutton, sister to his
master and friend Dr. Hutton, wrote on hearing of his
death, " My remembrance of him was when he was a
lovely boy about fifteen years of age, and kindly popped
over to make a morning call. I never can forget the

beauty of his countenance. It is really stamped upon my memory." At the time of his death, the Rev. P. H. Wicksteed was engaged in preparing the memoir of his father, the Rev. Charles Wicksteed, and in one of his father's early letters came upon the remark, " I never quarrelled with Frederick." The lifelong friendship of Frederick Swanwick and Charles Wicksteed, cousins and contemporaries in age, was formed in those days of bright boyhood.

In the autumn of 1826, Frederick Swanwick, then entering on his seventeenth year, became a student in the University of Edinburgh. He had already set his heart on the profession of his life, and pursued at Edinburgh those subjects which would form the best preparation for it. The principal of these were mathematics and natural philosophy, which he studied under Professor Leslie, and geology, which he studied under Professor Jameson. He devoted himself to his work with characteristic eagerness, and spared no effort to obtain as complete an equipment for his future career as his limited stay in the University permitted. He made use of the museum as well as of the other scientific advantages of the city ; and his introduction to the fields of scientific knowledge under those brilliant auspices probably laid the foundation of his profound conviction of the pre-eminent part the study of physical science is calculated to play in mental training. In after-life he often referred with pleasure to his sojourn as a student in Edinburgh.

By the summer of 1827 he had returned to his father's roof, and there prosecuted privately the study of mathe-

matics. The keen interest with which he was at this time
devoting himself to the study of civil engineering, is shown
by a letter to him, dated January 19, 1828, from his cousin
Mr. Thomas Wicksteed, who was a distinguished member of
the profession, for a number of years engineer of the "East
London Waterworks," and author of a work on the Cornish
Pumping Engine (1841). This letter had been elicited
by Frederick's inquiries as to numerous important enterprises
of engineering science at the time, and opens with the
encouraging and prophetic words, " My dear Frederick, I
am very much obliged to you for your clever, interesting,
and truly engineering letter, which has given not only me,
but one or two brother-engineers much pleasure; and,
although we know little or nothing about you, we augur
that you will be celebrated amongst us some day." The
inquiries which Mr. Wicksteed answers in his letter show that
Frederick Swanwick's eyes were thus early eagerly watching
all accounts of engineering work then being carried on in
any part of the country—*e.g.* the Hammersmith Suspension
Bridge, the new London Bridge, the Menai Bridge, the
substitution of a new foundation for the old one of the
Custom House, the St. Katharine Docks, etc. But the first
engineering work which fell under his own observation
was the construction of the Grosvenor Bridge at Chester
across the River Dee. It is a structure of great beauty,
and could then boast of having a stone arch with the largest
span of any in existence. The contractor and working
engineer, Mr. Trubshaw, was personally known to Mr.
Joseph Swanwick, and gave his son permission " to come

within the gates, and put his hand to the work." This kind offer was accepted by the lad with characteristically eager enthusiasm, which a severe cut upon the ankle from an adze he was using, confining him to his home for weeks, could not damp. This practical acquaintance with engineering operations, together with the contemporaneous study of mathematics, formed an invaluable preparation for his future calling.[1]

But fortune favoured him still further. To his great delight, through the help and good offices of an uncle, an elder brother of his father's, the opportunity of entering on his profession under the greatest engineer of the age now offered. Immediately after the completion of his nineteenth birthday he was articled as pupil to George Stephenson, who was then constructing the grand work of the time—the Liverpool and Manchester Railway. The indentures are dated October 5, 1829. By them "Frederick Swanwick bound himself apprentice to George Stephenson for four years and eight months from 5th October 1829 in the occupation or business of a civil engineer." Before he left home to enter upon the work of his life, Frederick's father, as he often remarked in later years, gave him two injunctions: "Never put off till to-morrow what you can do to-day;" and, "Remember, whatever is worth doing, is worth doing *well*." Another member of the family present at the time remembers that his father enforced the first maxim with the emphatic words: "I have suffered more from the ill effects of procrastination than from anything

[1] See Appendix A.

else," meaning that his position in life had been seriously injured by that defect.

George Stephenson's pupils at that time resided in the house of their master, and Mr. Swanwick was in later life wont to recall with great delight the happy relations in which they stood to their master. It was from materials which Mr. Swanwick supplied that Mr. Samuel Smiles drew up his account of these relations, which may therefore be quoted here :—

"His letters and reports written, and his sketches of drawings made and explained, the remainder of the evening was usually devoted to conversation with his wife and those of his pupils who lived under his roof, and constituted as it were part of the family.

"He then delighted to test the knowledge of his young companions, and to question them upon the principles of mechanics. If they were not quite 'up to the mark' on any point, there was no escaping detection by evasive or specious explanations on their part. These always met with the verdict of 'Ah, you know nought about it now; but think it over again and tell me the answer when you understand it.' . . . 'Learn for yourselves,—think for yourselves,' he would say, 'make yourselves masters of principles, —persevere, be industrious, and then there is no fear of you.' . . . Mr. Swanwick delights recalling to mind how seldom, if ever, a cross or captious word, or an angry look, marred the enjoyment of those evenings."[1]—

From the first, Frederick Swanwick adopted the motto

[1] Smiles' "Life of Stephenson" in *Lives of the Engineers*, vol. iii. p. 239.

of his English composition, "Whatsoever thy hand findeth to do, do it with thy might," and obeyed the parting injunctions of his father as he set forth from his roof. The habit of full and patient attention to every detail of his work was then formed, and to it he always ascribed a large portion of his success in his profession. He never allowed himself to be influenced by the notion of companions as to the indignity of some forms of work. It was an authentic lesson from the book of his own experience, therefore, when he used so emphatically in after-life to impress on young men entering on professions the importance of a complete personal mastery of *every* grade of work in their calling. Stephenson must at once have perceived that he had in his pupil a man who might be trusted absolutely to do whatever task had been assigned to him, and a man whom no difficulties could daunt. His quick eye must also have quickly perceived that his pupil possessed the intellectual qualifications and attainments which fitted him for important positions in his employment. Frederick had not been a year in his office before he made him his private secretary, in succession to Mr. Gooch,—a post which he retained until Stephenson removed his residence to Ashby-de-la-Zouch. In this position he not only enjoyed the inestimable advantage of watching the progress of the railway works, but the far greater one of being, as it were, behind the scenes of George Stephenson's thoughts, plans, experiments, and modes of carrying out their results. As Stephenson's secretary, he then " remarked " (to quote from Mr. Smiles' " Life of Stephenson ") "what in after years he could better appreciate—the clear, terse, and vigorous style of his dictation; there was nothing superfluous in it; but it was close, direct, and to the point—in short, it was thoroughly business-like." However acquired, whether in Stephenson's office or earlier, Mr. Swanwick's style possessed all these qualities of his master's dictation, with other merits which were peculiar to it. Like Stephenson, he saw clearly and grasped firmly the ideas he wished to express. In addition to this, an artistic sense of proportion and a fine sensitiveness to shades of meaning in words and phrases enabled him to present the matter in hand in the due relation of its parts and with perfect appropriateness of language. Thus his letters and reports, whether written in haste and without correction, or from drafts copiously altered, were always admirably done.

At the opening of the Manchester and Liverpool Railway, September 15, 1830, Frederick Swanwick was present, and drove on that occasion the Arrow, one of the engines which drew the first passenger train. In 1831 he was with Stephenson watching the construction of the Leicester and Swannington branch line, and was present at its opening.

What may be described as an epoch in his life was made by the assignment to him by Stephenson of the construction of a line between Whitby and Pickering. Before he had completed his twenty-second year he had surveyed this line and deposited his plans; and it is a striking proof of his confidence in his pupil that Stephenson gave him *carte blanche* as to the selection of the route and the formation of the line. "Though the line was but a single one, and for horse-power only, the route, the levels, and the strength of the works demanded precisely as much thought, care, and knowledge as for a double line of rails and for the heaviest locomotives. Indeed, the sharp curves that are both possible and economical on a horse railway require more delicate manipulation than the straight and more ordinary lines of rail." [1]

This work must have had great influence in more ways than one on Frederick Swanwick's life and character. It became with him a principle that it is responsibility which brings out the best that is in a man, and it was to this important and trying crisis in his life that he traced the origin of the conviction of its truth. From that time he did not himself shrink from responsibility, and in dealing with other men, either in his profession or in public life, it was with him a practical rule to throw upon some one competent person the full responsibility of an undertaking, and to expect the discharge of it. Stephenson's confidence, and the importance of the trust committed to him, called forth the utmost capacity, inventive resources and energies of his pupil. When he was surveying the line, as soon as the sun had risen till late at nightfall he was with his men amongst the woods and moors through which he had to carry his romantic road, enjoying to the full the battle with the great difficulties of his task as well as

---

[1] Mr. John Hutton.

the beauties of nature—animate and inanimate—through whose virgin recesses he struck the first iron pathway. In after-life he would refer with enthusiasm to the work and the scenery amid which it was done, and could never hear the cooing of the stock-dove without being vividly reminded of the Whitby and Pickering Railway.

The line was opened on May 26, 1836, when George Stephenson was present. Mr. Arnold Lupton[1] gives the following interesting description of its engineering aspects :—

"The total length of the railway was 24 miles; the rails were 40 lb. to the yard in 15 feet lengths, and were laid on stone sleepers, each containing 4 cubic feet. The greater part of the line had easy gradients, but there was one incline 1500 yards long with a gradient of 1 in 15. This was worked by water-power. The method of working was that of a self-acting incline common in mines, but here, differing from the case of a mine, the load was equal each way, and so there was attached to each train a water-tank; this was filled with water at the top of the incline, and its preponderating weight as it descended pulled the other train up the hill; arrived at the bottom, the water-tank was emptied and was sent up with the next train. The total cost of the line was £80,000, but with extra land purchased for probable enlargements, the cost was about £105,000, or £4,400 per mile. This is a good example of careful and conscientious work, no unnecessary

[1] *Memoirs of Deceased Members of the Chesterfield and Midland Counties Institution of Engineers.* London 1886.

expenditure, but a railway suited to the needs of the time, constructed at the smallest possible cost." [1]

But before this successful maiden effort of his professional career had reached completion, Frederick Swanwick had been called upon to undertake works of greater magnitude, involving still more serious responsibility. In the autumn of 1835 he received from George Stephenson the commission to lay out the North Midland Railway from Derby to Leeds. Mr. Stephenson and Mr. Swanwick went over the district on 5th and 6th of August, when the route was selected. Subsequently trial levels were taken by Mr. Swanwick and his assistants. On September 26th, Mr. Swanwick met George Stephenson at Sheffield to give directions for the survey. About the same time he made the survey of the York and North Midland and the Sheffield and Rotherham lines. It had also been one of the most important duties of the young engineer in 1836 to give evidence before the Committee of the House of Lords on the three lines which he had been surveying, as well as on the proposed line between Birmingham and Derby and others. Of this part of his work Mr. Arnold Lupton writes: "Mr. Swanwick acquired a great reputation for unfailing accuracy, as one who never lost a railway bill through any mistakes in plans or levels, and this at a time when in the struggle of rival schemes a most trifling and in itself unimportant error was sufficient to ensure the rejection of a bill." [2]

[1] Compare *Scenery of the Whitby and Pickering Railway*, chap. vi. p. 77. Appendix, p. 110.
[2] *Memoirs of Deceased Members, etc.*, p. 7.

A little incident which occurred on one of these occasions, very early in his professional life, may fitly be recorded here.   He had been examined before a Committee of the House of Lords, Lord Wharncliffe being the chairman, and, though every endeavour had been made to baffle and disconcert him, had exhibited that complete mastery of all the details which, combined with readiness and nerve, always characterized his advocacy of a bill. But when the proceedings were at an end and he had gathered up his papers to go, he could not find his hat. " What are you looking for, Mr. Swanwick ? " asked Lord Wharncliffe.   " My hat, your lordship."   " Oh, never mind your hat.   You haven't lost your head at all events," was his lordship's reply.   This unexpected compliment from the noble chairman, who was personally opposed to the bill, was encouraging to the young engineer after the badgering of the day, and before he had had an opportunity of knowing his own strength.

The Act for the North Midland Railway was obtained in 1836, and Mr. Swanwick became acting engineer in its construction, with the full responsibility of the position, this case forming no exception to George Stephenson's rule of devolving upon the man in charge almost the entire work and responsibility of the construction of a line.[1]   To him was assigned the laying out of the line, the preparation of the plans and specifications of all the work, and not only this but also a good deal of

---

[1] Two letters from Mr. Stephenson to Mr. Swanwick, printed in Appendix B, are indicative of this.

the organization and superintendence in detail of important portions of the work in progress—in fact, many of the duties now entrusted to the contractor.[1]

In the discharge of such nearly unlimited responsibilities Mr. Swanwick worked night and day, and showed an almost omnipresent vigilance. Mr. Hutton says that "during the progress of the works of the Clay Cross Tunnel he would snatch a hasty dinner late in the evening while his gig was waiting at the door, drive the seven miles from Whittington to Clay Cross, don his tunnel dress, and surprise the night gangs by his appearance amongst them." [2]

The construction of the 72 miles of the North Midland line from Derby to Leeds took four years to accomplish. It was a great work, admirably executed. Mr. Hutton thus describes it: "It is unnecessary to tell the thousands of Englishmen who have travelled over this line that it pierces the backbone of England, tunnels beneath its coal measures, and crosses many times some of its principal rivers. The works are therefore exceedingly heavy, and Mr. Swanwick devoted untiring energy to make them permanent and absolutely sound, at the least possible cost, and without sacrificing reasonable beauty of design. It has been said, and with truth, that no railway works in England exceed those of this line in strength and durability."

The year 1840 saw the opening of the North Midland

[1] An interesting description of this part of an engineer's duties in those days is given by Mr. Swanwick himself in his speech at the Stephenson Centenary. See Appendix C, and comp. App. D.

[2] *Proceedings of the Institute, etc.*, p. 4.

line, on June 30th.   A great work had been successfully
accomplished, a name had been made, and a singularly
prosperous career fully opened.   But Mr. Swanwick's was
an unusually social and affectionate nature, and however
devoted he might be to his professional calling, it could
not absorb the more tender and ideal instincts of his heart.
He had always shown himself to be the most affectionate
of sons and brothers, and the kindest and most faithful
of friends ; and notwithstanding the paucity of written
reminiscences of the life of the man as distinct from the
busy occupations of the engineer, eloquent signs crop up
testifying that his heart was not wholly given to the
construction of railways.

From 1836 to 1837 his headquarters had been at
Norton Lees, near the pretty hamlet of Norton, about four
miles from Sheffield, known in wider circles as the birth-
place of the sculptor Chantrey.   In 1837 he removed
thence to Whittington, to which he induced his father and
mother and sister to come, to share his home.   He also
persuaded his maiden aunts, the Misses Wicksteed, his first
schoolmistresses, to take up their abode in an adjoining
house.   His father and mother lived with him the rest of
their days.   Mr. Swanwick died in September 1841, and
Mrs. Swanwick, December 1845.

An old record of the early days of his settlement at
Whittington, from a friend then living at Norton, gives a
charming glimpse of him when the family party, as sometimes happened, drove over to Norton on the Sunday, the
minister and his family being old friends.   " How pleasant

it was to have the family from Whittington join in the worship of the little chapel at Norton ! . . . . How genial he was to all, and how loving, tender, and respectful to his old aunts! He was indeed a ray of sunshine as he passed." In those days of early ambition, as in his later life, he found the deepest satisfaction and delight in the society of cultivated people, in aiding every good work of human enlightenment, and in ministering to the happiness of dear friends and relatives. Having established himself in his home at Whittington, the one thing wanting to complete the domestic happiness was the companionship and help of a wife able to respond to all the finer and deeper tendencies of his nature. This happy consummation was attained on July 21, 1840, a little less than a month after the opening of the North Midland Railway, by his marriage with Elizabeth Drayton, fourth child of Mr. William Drayton, of Leicester. The union was one of the happiest, and brought to his home and life a son and daughter. In due course grandchildren followed, and in the young friends and relatives so frequently at his house, the tender delight of his sympathetic nature in the life and happiness of children and young people—a delight which to the very last he felt—found full gratification.

One word as to Whittington, (dear to so many as Mr. Swanwick's home !) the place where he had chosen to fix his abode, and the scene not only of his happy domestic life and boundless hospitality, but also of some of his public work in one of its chief directions — namely, education. The village is three miles north of Chesterfield, prettily situated above the valley of the Rother, which expands at its feet, while at the back lies a fine stretch of hilly country, running away to the Derbyshire moors. It was itself once part of those moors, and this long after the Earl of Devonshire and his compatriots met at the Cock and Pynot, in the " Plotting Chamber," a little cottage adjoining Mr. Swanwick's property, to concoct the glorious Revolution of 1688. When Mr. Swanwick chose the place for his home, it was still a pretty quiet village quite in the country and amid the beauties of nature, removed sufficiently far from the noise and smoke and other hideous features of the new coal and iron industries which railroads were destined rapidly to develop. Of the continuous lines of houses which now for nearly three miles connect Old Whittington with Chesterfield, there were then but two or three, and they good-looking buildings of Derbyshire stone. The fine valley of the Rother, which is now black and ugly with the coal-pits and iron-works of New Whittington and Staveley, was then in quiet and almost untarnished loveliness. Whittington itself, which had in 1881 a population of 7271, numbered then but 900 souls, and all the hamlets and villages round about (where any then existed) were sweet country spots, in which a true lover of nature, such as Mr. Swanwick was, could feast his soul on her sights and sounds without disturbance. The house and grounds which were to be the permanent scene of his domestic life, were at first modest and unpretentious, illustrating in this respect one great principle of his life—never to be an engineer or builder whose work should anywhere lack the fulfilment of its design. Driving up to Whittington for the first time, when he was in search of a place of residence in the neighbourhood, for his guidance this description was given him, " It is the red house in the big field." The charm of the view and the advantages of the situation and extent of ground were recognised by him at a glance, and the decision to take the place was immediately arrived at. Shortly afterwards it was purchased, and in course of time surrounding land, and in subsequent years of greater leisure further alterations of the house and grounds were made. Thus he saw the place grow under his hands.

The next ten years of his life after the founding of his home (1840–1850), like the previous ten years, were devoted to his profession with characteristic energy. He continued resident engineer of the Midland Railway until 1844, and then took charge of the company's fresh projections, piloting the bills through Parliament, and afterwards superintending the construction of the lines. Amongst these were the Nottingham and Mansfield, Nottingham and Lincoln, the Erewash Valley, the Pinxton and Mansfield, the Junction between the Midland and the Sheffield and Manchester at Sheffield. He was also engaged in preparing bills for several railways which were not made for some years afterwards.

The strain which this parliamentary and engineering work—necessarily carried on simultaneously through part of the year—must have involved was immense. It is difficult now to conceive how it could be borne, and that any constitution could have stood it, and survived the trial permanently unimpaired.

The pressure of work reached a climax during the weeks immediately preceding the 30th November each year, the date by which all proposals for new lines (the Acts for which were to be obtained in the ensuing session of Parliament) had to be deposited with the public authority. The completion of the necessary plans was often accomplished only by a total disregard of the distinction of day and night on the part of all concerned, and especially of the chief. He has been known to work under such circumstances for a whole week without sleep. Without the possession of the invaluable faculty of sleeping soundly when his work was done, he could never have performed such feats of endurance. On one occasion, after a week without sleep, having finished the work in hand, he lay down, tired out, and fell soundly asleep at his inn at Doncaster, while waiting for the post-chaise which was to take him to the Rotherham station. He was lifted into the chaise, with instructions to the driver to hand him over to the guard at Rotherham, who was to deliver him to the station-master at Chesterfield, who again was to send him on to Whittington. When he arrived at home he knew nothing of what had happened since he fell asleep at Doncaster. His perfectly abstemious habits enabled him to enjoy as an excellent joke the report that " Mr. Swanwick had been taken home dead drunk ! "

As Mr. John Hutton says, " His note-books, letter-books, and accounts indicate sufficiently his incessant activity, the almost inconceivable distances he compassed in each twenty‑four hours, — his various offices, London, the different works in progress, and his home for brief intervals. His assistants used to think him ubiquitous. Occasionally the rapidity of his movements puzzled and perplexed them, for he was not conscious, judging by the amount of work he had himself got through, how short a time had passed since he had last given his directions, and how unable they were therefore to produce the finished work which he had hoped to find accomplished." [1]

By way of advice to others, Mr. Swanwick would some‑ times refer to his rule, on lying down to rest at night, of never allowing the brain to busy itself with prospective plans of work, but of reserving till the morning the thinking out of any matter which required all the fresh energies of the mind. This rule had been adopted by him when his professional responsibilities were growing heavy. After having been warned by experience of the evil consequences of its non‑observance, he adhered to it with characteristic self‑command.

The work of surveying for projected lines had often to be done in the face of great difficulties, which arose from the determined opposition of large landowners whose estates were about to be invaded. In such cases surveys had sometimes to be made in the darkness of the night, not infrequently in frost and snow, by the aid of lanterns, " and many were the adventures and escapes, which old engineers love to recall to each other, of those days of

[1] Compare Appendix D.

engineering exploits."[1]   Mr. Swanwick, however, seldom
spoke of his own doings, and we owe the following interesting story of one of these adventures in which he was
prominent, to the fact that a distinguished man who had
made a powerful impression upon him was concerned in it.

Mr. Swanwick had been making surveys for a projected
railway in the neighbourhood of Wakefield, and one of
the alternative routes passed through the park of the
famous naturalist Waterton.   This was one of the cases in
which the survey had to be made at night, though a route
not passing through the great naturalist's park was
ultimately determined on.   Still it was deemed desirable
to bespeak his goodwill for the projected line, and Mr.
Swanwick, accompanied by the solicitor, proceeded to call
on him.   Their ring at the door brought Mr. Waterton in
person, leaving them no opportunity of giving their names.
They began at once to announce their business, and
described the proposed line.   " We have come to ask for
your approval and support of the line, Mr. Waterton;
what answer may we give ? "

" Say," he exclaimed, " that I am damnably opposed ! "

" Is that the answer you would wish me to record ? "
said the solicitor with suave courtesy.

" Well," said Waterton, " if you would promise to smash
up that d—d canal,[2] I might give you my support."

[1] Mr. John Hutton.
[2] The canal passed close to the park gates, and, in consequence of a series
of locks occurring just there, the bargemen were often loitering about,
particularly on Sundays, and causing the naturalist great annoyance by
trespassing in his park.

Mr. Swanwick intimated that though they could not undertake to ruin the canal, the railway would no doubt be a formidable rival to it.

On being shown the plans, Mr. Waterton was taken aback at seeing a survey across his park included; and, in a suppressed voice, as if speaking of an offence too black to be mentioned aloud, he said, " I have been *told* that Mr. Swanwick and his men were actually in my park making a survey !"—at this point his rage mastering him,—"By God, if I had seen him, I would have shot him ! "

" Allow me to introduce Mr. Swanwick," said the solicitor with courteous ceremony.

Waterton recovering himself, " Well, I cannot tell what I might not have done. I should have been so enraged at the thought of a railway coming through my park, where no gun is ever heard, where my birds live as securely as in the primeval forests."

Waterton then proceeded to show his visitors his interesting collection of stuffed birds and animals, calling special attention at last to a creature of apparently composite type, half monkey, half another animal, and appealed to them with apparent indignation, " They say I have made up this creature; I ask you, is it possible ? " Waterton also spoke of his wife whom he had lost, and seems to have opened out on this occasion in an unusual manner.

After nearly twenty years of such intense application to his profession as has been indicated in the above faint outline, Mr. Swanwick began to prepare for retirement.

In this resolve we cannot fail to see an illustration of his
characteristic practical wisdom, and an act of obedience to the
finer instincts of his soul, which taught him to subordinate
even the chosen calling of his life to life's higher interests.
This is one of the lessons which his career has to teach
to busy men.   His success had been great, and he was
absolutely free not only from the weakness and the vice of
avarice, but from the error of bounding life by his profession.   Public duties, his family, travel, books, the
society of his friends,—these and kindred duties and
attractions had during his busiest years always powerfully
appealed to the primary tendencies of his nature.
Accordingly about 1850, instead of undertaking fresh
professional work, involving a greater sacrifice of home
and other ties than before, he gradually retired from his
profession.   He was then still a comparatively young man,
in the full enjoyment of bodily health and mental vigour.

We have now to indicate the outline of his life in his
retirement.

While in the press and throng of professional work Mr.
Swanwick had taken a warm interest and an active share
in promoting such useful institutions of the neighbourhood
as the Mechanics' Institute, the Operatives' Library, the
Infant, the Industrial, and the British Schools in Chesterfield, and had begun to devote earnest attention to the
means of elementary education in Whittington.   With the
leisure which freedom from professional duties brought,
these and other public institutions commanded his constant
assistance and support.

But before passing to the details of his public labours, we must not omit incidentally to observe that when he had laid aside the work of his profession, his strong sense of right and of the obligations connected with property would not suffer him to look idly on, or shirk any responsibility, however small others might deem it, when injustice appeared to him to be involved in the action of public companies with which he was connected. An instance of this was the laborious effort (happily successful) which he made with the view of ending a really disgraceful litigation on the part of the Edinburgh and Glasgow Railway Company with the Stirling and Dunfermline Railway Company, in 1857. While some fellow-shareholders in the former company, disgusted with what the *Railway Times* described as "a scandal," sold out their shares, he considered such a course a dereliction of duty, and not only made a vigorous protest against the action of the chairman and directors of the Edinburgh and Glasgow Company, but by dint of great exertion succeeded in getting a meeting of the shareholders of that Company, the result of his efforts being an amalgamation of the contending Companies on a fairer basis, and the end of the scandalous litigation.

Amongst the specially philanthropic institutions in which Mr. Swanwick took an active and constant interest, was the Chesterfield and North Derbyshire Hospital. He was for many years vice - president of the board of governors, contributed to the funds, and took a regular and efficient share in the inspection of the wards and the

general management of the institution.   His advice was
highly valued in the matter of the investment of the
endowments; for though it was not known to the public
that he had never in his life made a bad investment, his
reputation was great as a sagacious business man, with
a special knowledge of railway property.[1]   He attended
the board meetings with great regularity, and would
either so arrange his absence from home as not to clash
with them, or travel long distances in order to be in his
place.   On his visits through the wards, his kindly
interest in each case, the cheery and tender tones of his
voice, and the sweetness of his face, must have brought
comfort to many a poor sufferer.

It was in the year 1869 that Mr. Swanwick was asked
to accept the position of a Justice of the Peace for the
county of Derby.   With characteristic conscientiousness, he
hesitated for a time, under the feeling that men who had
not had a legal training were not qualified for the
magisterial office.   When he had become convinced that it
was his duty to assume the responsibility, he spared no
pains to qualify himself, by a careful study of the laws which
he had to assist in administering, and of each case as it
came before him.   He was soon valued as one of the most
painstaking, independent, and just of the magistrates of the
county.   He made it a great point that the penalties inflicted
should bear as just a proportion to the heinousness of the

---

[1] It is true, a very unprofitable investment of some of the funds of the
hospital in railway shares was in one instance made when he was one of three
to whom the matter had been entrusted.   But it is personally known to me,
that it was against his distinct advice and in his absence that this was done.

offence committed and the circumstances of the offender as the law would admit. His own scarcely veiled contempt for the pleasures of "sport," with a good degree of tenderness for some of the poor men whom gamekeepers are apt sweepingly to class amongst confirmed poachers, rendered his presence on the bench the one hope and comfort of those who were charged with being "in pursuit of game."

In politics Mr. Swanwick was a decided and staunch Liberal—in this respect a true son of his father. He took a very active, prominent, and influential part as a leader of his party in Derbyshire. Indeed, if he had not made it distinctly understood that it was quite out of the question to think of it, he would have been nominated in 1880 one of the two candidates for the North-Eastern Division of Derbyshire. He was particularly active in the election of 1868, and portions of a speech which he delivered then as chairman at one of the Liberal candidates' meetings at Whittington are given in an Appendix,[1] as illustrating the breadth of his Liberalism and his style of speaking.

Only those who had the good fortune to work with Mr. Swanwick as an ally can form any idea of the energy and enthusiasm which he threw into a political contest, while he preserved in an unusual degree the most perfect good temper, never descending on any occasion to anything approaching "personalities," and keeping on the best of terms with his numerous Conservative friends. To the very last, though his strength was fast failing, he retained his deep interest in political affairs. Though he did not live

[1] Appendix E.

to see the election of 1885, he watched keenly, as on former occasions, the arrangements for the contest, and as late as 6th October, in reply to the request to take the chair at a meeting in favour of the Liberal candidate, Admiral Egerton, he wrote :—

" I find that I must relinquish the hope of being present at the meeting at Whittington to-morrow, as this is peremptorily forbidden me.   It is a great disappointment to me not to meet my fellow-electors on this occasion, to join in the expression of confidence in Mr. Gladstone and the late Cabinet and the Liberal candidate, Admiral Egerton, who has for so many years given such loyal service to the party and to the constituency which he has so faithfully represented.   I trust that at the forthcoming election we shall return Admiral Egerton by an overwhelming majority."

But the field of public and philanthropic labour which Mr. Swanwick delighted most of all to work in, was that of education in the widest sense of the word.   Here he was an enthusiast, and, as we have seen, before his retirement, in the press and throng of his professional career, he took an earnest interest in several educational institutions of Whittington and Chesterfield.   He had unbounded faith in human progress, and in the spread of knowledge and mental culture as the chief instruments of it.   When the movement for the establishment of Mechanics' Institutes and Operatives' Libraries commenced, he was a zealous supporter of it.   In Whittington he kept up an excellent village library, and in Chesterfield it was mainly by his help that an Operatives'

Library, with a very capital selection of books, was started and maintained for many years. He was one of the principal promoters of the Chesterfield Free Library, and assisted in its establishment by a large subscription. In connection with the Mechanics' Institutes, he used all his influence to get into the neighbourhood the best lecturers obtainable. On these occasions, and similar ones in later years, his house was the home of the lecturers, and he was in the habit of inviting his neighbours to meet there such men as Emerson, George Dawson, and Dr. Carpenter. When the more recent movement of University extension was started, he heartily and liberally encouraged it. From the time when he was first able to direct his attention to education, he spared no pains to acquire clear views as to its true nature and the best methods of imparting it. He sought the acquaintance of distinguished educationalists, and took the warmest interest in their work. He was in the habit of carefully studying the Government reports on elementary and higher education. Even in his busiest days he visited some of the best elementary schools in the country, either to see the most convenient school-buildings, or to be present when able masters were instructing or examining their classes. Some of his experiences on these visits he never forgot, and would in after-life relate them to his friends. Two of these may find a place here.

Wishing to hear the eminent educationalist Mr. Ellis give a lesson to a large class in one of the elementary schools in London, as he was in the habit of doing, Mr. Swanwick went in search of the school, and in consequence of misdirection found himself in the wrong one. The master, however, intimated that he would be delighted that his visitor should stay to hear the lesson on grammar which he was then about to give to a class of pupil-teachers. The kind permission was used, and the class proceeded to parse Mark Antony's address, "Friends, Romans, countrymen, lend me your ears! The evil that men do lives after them," etc. All went swimmingly until the word "do" was reached. Every possible account of the troublesome verb was given by the class, but without satisfying the master, who grew more and more impatient at each fresh failure. At last he himself supplied the answer, quite taking away the breath of his astonished visitor. "Don't you see, boys! *verb emphatic:* DO *lives.*" It was not necessary for Mr. Swanwick to stay longer in that school, and he resumed his search for Mr. Ellis, whom he soon found. He was giving a lesson to the head class of boys. They had been taken in a body to a tannery, and were being questioned by Mr. Ellis as to the object and rationale of the various processes of tanning, in a way that struck Mr. Swanwick as admirably adapted to stimulate the boys' powers of thought as well as of observation. Then followed a lesson on political economy, and the circumstances likely to create a demand for an article were brought under consideration. The question was put to the class, "Would it be good policy to send skates to Brazil?" which received the general answer "No!" Pursuing the consideration, Mr. Ellis selected a very bright and intelligent-looking boy to tell him "Why." "Because there are plenty of them there."

Surprised at such an answer, Mr. Ellis went on to ask the boy if he knew whether water froze there, and similar questions, trying to bring him to discover for himself his error, but all in vain. At length the schoolmaster went up to Mr. Ellis, and said in a low voice, "The boy's father is a *fishmonger !*" which explained the mystery. But the curious and striking illustration of Mr. Ellis's patient method of drawing out a boy's thinking power made a deep impression on Mr. Swanwick.

It was in connection with the elementary education of the parish of Whittington that Mr. Swanwick worked most assiduously, and with most tangible results. The field was an expanding one; and, with the co-operation of his neighbours and the help of the Charity Commissioners, he was permitted to see the growing wants of the population in this important matter fully met.

When Mr. Swanwick first came to reside in Whittington, the population was under a thousand; at the census of 1881 it was 7271. By the extension of the coal and iron industries, Whittington at length became three villages, under the names of Old Whittington, New Whittington, and Whittington Moor. When he first took up his abode in the place, it could boast of nothing better than dameschools. There existed, indeed, an old charity, left in the seventeenth century, part of which ought to have been employed in paying a schoolmaster. There was also a schoolbuilding, part of the same endowment; but it was shut up, and fast falling into ruin. The last entry of payment to a schoolmaster occurs in 1841. In 1848 a new schoolhouse was built, for which Mr. Swanwick gave the site and a very liberal contribution in money ; and, as a trustee, he earnestly endeavoured, in the face of much opposition and litigation on the part of a denominational party, which soon arose, to preserve the school free from all sectarian trammels. After much trouble and conflict, this object and the utilization of the endowments in the promotion of elementary education were secured in 1857 by a scheme "allowed by the Master of the Rolls."   A conscience clause was attached to this scheme, which provided that no scholar should be required to learn any catechism or other religious formulary, or attend any Sunday school or other place of worship, to which his parents should on religious grounds object.   The Bible was to be read daily to or by all the scholars whose parents did not on religious grounds object. When the Schools Inquiry Commissioner for the North Midland Division reported on the school in 1864 there were about 130 children in attendance, mostly children of miners, who left the school at the early age of nine.   The school accommodation was rapidly becoming insufficient, and the opening up of the mineral wealth of the district both increased the need of new schools and the value of the endowment.   Mr. Swanwick energetically seized upon the twofold opportunity.   By a new scheme of the Charity Commissioners in 1874, the governors of the charity were allowed to spend £5000 in providing sites and buildings for schools at New Whittington and at Whittington Moor, and to add to the school premises at Old Whittington.

Scope was thus given for the gratification of Mr.

Swanwick's enthusiasm in the cause of education. It became one of the laborious occupations of his last years to assist in meeting the educational wants of the three Whittingtons. As chairman of the board of governors he spared himself no pains, and in some cases no annoyances, to provide the most commodious, well-arranged, and healthy school-buildings and premises, himself contributing land and money for the purpose. He took great pains to find able masters and mistresses. And as a characteristic of his loyalty to the undenominational principle, it ought not to be left unmentioned, that though he was a most influential chairman of a board of governors the large majority of whom were, like himself, Dissenters, he never allowed the religious denomination to which the candidates for the post of master or mistress might belong to be inquired into previous to their election. As a fact, the masters and mistresses actually appointed were more frequently members of the Established Church than Dissenters. His earnest and prolonged efforts in the establishment and management of these schools were crowned with large success. The three schools took a foremost place amongst the best elementary schools in the kingdom. In the year 1881 there were in attendance at them 1111 children, and the grant earned from Government reached the large total of £917. With the endowment and the children's pence, this large grant met the expenses of the schools, and enabled the governors to offer salaries sufficiently high to secure the best teaching power. The boon of such schools to the three villages was beyond all price, and Mr. Swanwick enjoyed not only the satisfaction of witnessing the beneficial effects of his labours, but also of knowing that the people on whose behalf they were given appreciated them.

On the subject of middle-class and higher education, in which, as has already been said, Mr. Swanwick took an earnest interest, he held very definite views, and views which were in advance of his age, though they are now gradually finding more general acceptance. It was more especially as to the place of Latin and Greek in the general and compulsory curriculum of the second-class and higher schools that he zealously advocated opinions not commonly held. On this point there has happily been preserved a statement of his views written by himself. It is addressed to his cousin, Miss Anna Swanwick, and was followed by a lengthy letter referring to points which had been passed over in it. The paper was not written for any other eyes than Miss Swanwick's, and the letter was even less *prepared.* Yet the two present so well his views on that matter that Miss Swanwick has kindly allowed them to be inserted here. The preliminary note accompanying the statement explains the occasion of it.

"WHITTINGTON, CHESTERFIELD,
Feb. 10, 1884.

"MY DEAR COUSIN,—Mary mentioned that you wished I would send you some remarks on the study of Latin and Greek.

"On asking her last night about it, she said that she

thought there was a meeting on Tuesday, before which date she thought you would wish to receive anything I had to send. I did not on going to bed last night feel that I could do any justice to the subject; but this morning a rash impulse seized me, and I sat down and wrote the accompanying very crude and desultory remarks; and it is only the arrival of post-time that I fear procures your release from my lucubrations.

" I ought, no doubt, to put it in the fire, without troubling you with it. I must request you to assign to it the fate it ought to receive at my hands. It is, too, I know, disgracefully illegible, and I must beg you to regard it as a very insufficient sketch of what another hand could present of the merits of the question.

" In haste, I am, yours affectionately,

" F. SWANWICK."

" What value attaches to the study of Latin and Greek in the education of the people ?

" The study of the histories of the Latin and Greek nations is admittedly of high interest, and a knowledge of them must be obtained primarily through a knowledge of the respective languages. This knowledge has been acquired by a large number of persons who have made us acquainted by translations with the writings and history of these nations. These translations, it will be admitted, give us a more accurate knowledge of those writings and history than can be obtained by the bulk of the people by very many years of close study of the languages. So that we get the particular information with the least expenditure of time withdrawn from other studies. This proposition will, no doubt, be granted, just as it is granted that a sufficient knowledge of the history of other and older nations, and of the thoughts and systems of their leading men, may be obtained without a study of their respective languages, *e.g.* Hebrew and the various dialects of the East. Those who attach the highest importance to the books of the Old Testament do not contend that every one should be acquainted with Hebrew, or be acquainted with all the languages of the East, in order to obtain a sufficient knowledge of the systems of Buddha, Confucius, and other leaders of thought of the Eastern world.

"But it may be said the study of the two ancient languages of Greece and Rome is a means of intellectual training; that in them are found the roots of a large portion of our own and of the Continental languages, and so many of our scientific terms are derived from them; that they have a refining influence; that they are associated not only with the history and literature, but also with the mythology, and therefore with the art, of the ancient world; that all our statesmen and eminent men have been brought up under a system in which these languages formed the basis and a large part of their early education; and that the intelligence of the middle and upper classes is traceable to the existence of this system.

"Taking the last of these claims first, it may be replied, that the revival of letters necessarily took place in connection with the only literature which existed—that of the ancients

—and that these languages, and especially the Latin, was necessarily or naturally the medium of instruction; that this system became an essential element in the earlier grammar schools and universities, and that the heads and patrons of these schools naturally perpetuated a system with which alone they were acquainted.   And it may be reasonably claimed that the intelligence of the so-called educated class has not been *in consequence*, but *in spite* of their educational system.   Just as when the subject of the repeal of the corn laws was discussed, the plea in their defence was, ' Great Britain is a great and prosperous nation ; Great Britain has its corn laws; its prosperity is therefore owing to its corn laws.'   The answer was and is, Great Britain is flourishing, *not in consequence* of, but *in spite* of her corn laws.   All sorts of disaster were predicted as sure to follow the repeal of these laws; so now, in the matter of education, any serious interference with the old grammar school and university system is denounced.   It is declared that if you remove the old landmarks we shall be left on a beaconless sea.   Remove the old foundations, and no sound superstructure can be raised.   Take away the study of ancient languages as the principal occupation of school-life, and it will be succeeded by a dilettante system—a system of superficialities and cram, without digestion—a little of all the ' ologies,' with an entire absence of mental gymnastics— a puffing up of our youth (and of their parents) with the notion that they are highly and widely educated, when they have in reality only a superficial smattering.

   " Such are the phantoms which are to prevent our open-

ing our eyes to the defects and evils of the present system.
It is monstrous to suppose that those who have thought on
the subject do not recognise the absolute necessity of com-
bining the *acquisitional* with the *educational*.

"We contend that the present system of education is
not that best calculated to promote intellectual vigour;
that the acquisition of language is not the end, but simply
a means of assisting to strengthen the powers and to obtain
and accumulate information. We contend that a judicious
use of our *modern* 'classics' will best effect the cardinal
objects of stimulating thought and aiding clearness of style,
of storing the memory and exciting the imagination. How
many lives would be enriched, if, instead of spending the
best years of their youth in acquiring the ancient languages
(which in ninety-nine cases out of a hundred—nay, nine
hundred and ninety-nine cases out of a thousand, never
yield in after-life any gratification or resource), the same
years were spent in acquiring an intimacy with modern
classical authors, essayists, and poets; in learning, *linguisti-
cally*, if not grammatically (in the technical sense), modern
languages, thus obtaining access not only to foreign authors
but also to foreigners and their countries; in getting a com-
prehensive knowledge of the history and institutions of other
nations, including an insight into the Constitutional history
of our own, and some intimacy with the principles and the
practice of our own laws, of which almost every one is all but
absolutely ignorant; in getting some knowledge of some
at least of the various branches of natural history and of
applied science, of human physiology, of those laws and

facts which bear upon bodily health and hygiene, and on the study of music and art and architecture. Economize our time and improve our methods of instruction as we may, this wide field cannot be *fully* cultivated; but if it were done only to the extent that is practicable, we might succeed in creating tastes and aspirations which would save the vacuous minds of our youth from the temptations to which they are exposed when launched into the world unarmoured by any higher tastes. The upper middle and upper classes might possibly feel that, however important physical exercise is, there might occasionally be leisure for something else than hunting, shooting, boating, cricketing, gambling, and other modes of killing time. Our landed proprietors might feel that they were not utterly ignorant of every science bearing on the cultivation of their land and the management of their property. If it be said that only a smattering can be obtained of many of the subjects indicated, I say that it is better to have a smattering than no knowledge. 'A little knowledge is a dangerous thing' only when it leads its possessor to fancy that he has more than he really has; and it frequently happens that it is only after a glimpse of a subject has been obtained that the student's taste for pursuing it is developed.

"Returning for a moment to the suggestion that Latin and Greek help in the study of modern languages, and in understanding scientific terms, I would ask, how often is their study useful to the traveller abroad? Who is it that has to help the English travelling party in France? Not the father or brother who has spent so many years in acquiring Latin, but the wife or sister who has never learnt a word of Latin. How deeply does the English traveller in Germany —in entire ignorance of its language—regret that some portion of the time given to the study of the ancient languages was not given to the acquisition of a knowledge of German !

"With regard to scientific terms, the nomenclature is readily acquired and classified, and it is idle to contend that years must be given for the sake of acquiring this facility. The druggist's apprentice's knowledge of Latin terms used in his business is probably more accurate than that of the senior optime.

"But, it may be asked, are grammar and philology to be discarded from the field of study? Certainly not. We require specialists who, possessing long leisure and natural taste and faculty, will not only enrich us with translations, but will master the whole subject, and out of the completeness of their knowledge will enlighten and interest those who must be content to take much of this kind of information at second hand; for the accomplished philologist will be able to assign a root or origin, not only to the words traceable to the ancient languages, but also to those traceable to modern languages, thus making the subject rich in instruction and interest.

"It is true that some modification of the old curriculum of study has been effected of late years, but I submit that it is not sufficient, and that the change ought to be accelerated."

"WHITTINGTON, *Feb.* 28, 1884.

"MY DEAR COUSIN,—I have not thanked you for your last kind note of the 15th of February. The subject of education in early life is so important a one that I ask your indulgence to refer to it again.

"I quite allow that when the conditions you name of *'facility in acquiring'* and *'ample time'* coexist, such an intimate knowledge of an ancient language may be acquired as will enable the student to realize and assimilate the thoughts of an author, and then to give to the world the exact meaning and spirit of the author in a modern language. To such a student this work must be of especial interest, but it is not the work which belongs to the thousand, but to *one only in ten thousand*, who thus reap the advantage of the labour and skill of the one thoroughly competent student.

"There remains the question as to the value—acquisitionally and educationally and disciplinarily—of the study to those who can do little more than acquire a smattering or empirical knowledge of the ancient languages. The discussion of this question is attended with the serious difficulty that the great body of educationalists have been brought up under the long-established curriculum of our public schools and universities, so that thus a serious inertia has first to be encountered. Happily, however, there are many persons who, notwithstanding their early training, have felt compelled to denounce the existing system. Amongst those who have distinguished themselves in this way, there occur to me amongst public men the names of Robert Lowe, Grant Duff, Dr. Hodgson, Dr. Thompson, the present Archbishop of York,—all men of high 'classical' attainments, who have on various public occasions written and spoken strongly on the subject. The Archbishop of York, I recollect, in addressing a public school said that the time would come when the world would look back with amazement at the present system of education, which gives to the ancient languages the prominence they hold. He has spoken in the same strong terms in Manchester and elsewhere; so have Grant Duff and Lowe. Dr. Hodgson, himself an accomplished scholar, and with wide practical experience as a teacher in two of the largest schools in our great towns, denounced the present system most trenchantly. An article of his in the *Westminster Review,* which appeared more than twenty years ago, attracted great attention. It appeared anonymously, but it struck me as so admirable that I obtained the name of the author, and then sought his acquaintance. He retained his strong opinions on the subject to the day of his death, and was considering the suggestion which had been made, that he should collect and republish the papers which he had written on the topic.

"I may here mention that a very able article on the subject appeared in the *Edinburgh Review* of July 1864. I was anxious to know who was the powerful ally, and wrote to the editor to ask if there was any objection to his name being given privately. This, however, he said was contrary to the practice, and that the author was a man of high standing.

"In the case of the largest public middle-class school in the kingdom—Edward the Sixth's in Birmingham—I know that one of the most intelligent masters expressed to the then headmaster his conviction that they were not doing justice to the large number of boys under their care by giving so much of their time to the ancient languages. After the discussion had continued for some time, the headmaster said, ' My good friend, we will not pursue the subject ; you and I can teach nothing else.'

" I recollect that on one occasion a long conversation I had with a university graduate engaged in tuition was brought to a close by his remark, ' The Church is placed over us in matters of religious belief, and the Universities are placed over us in matters of education,'—a dictum which rendered any further discussion useless.

" When the Commission which was appointed more than twenty years ago to consider the regulations under which candidates for service in India should be admitted, of which Commission Lord Macaulay was chairman, the importance of giving a more liberal education than that given in the public schools and universities was discussed, and most cogent reasons were assigned for great changes in the curriculum ; but the report concluded by saying that it would not be fair to the older universities to make any material change. This conclusion was expressed, as far as I recollect, in this naked manner. It was not suggested that there should be a gradual change, and that it would not be fair to examinees coming from the universities to subject them to an examination for which their school and college life had not prepared them, and that the system must be gradually changed so as to embrace a wider field of instruction. No such suggestion was made, but it seemed to be assumed that the university system was stereotyped, and must be disturbed by no rude hand, though the interests of our Indian Empire were at stake.

" I do not know whether you are acquainted with the Report of the Public School Commission, who made their report in 1864. It was composed of eminent men, such as Clarendon, Lyttleton, Devon (not Devonshire), Stafford Northcote, Thompson, the present Archbishop of York, and others, but no man of scientific eminence was upon it. They examined a great number of witnesses, men of science included. The inquiry embraced, as you may recollect, the nine public schools then prominent. The report expresses the utter failure of the system of public school education (as regards the large proportion of those who go to the universities) even to give a fair amount of knowledge of the two ancient languages.

" The Commissioners venture to recommend that the modern languages and natural science should have some attention, but they evidently cannot break through the trammels of their own early associations, and the long-established practice of the schools and universities. They found in one of these schools an endowment of 'classical' studies in scholarships, etc., of about £1300, out of which modern languages were allotted the liberal amount of £50, and natural science a like amount of £50.

" The Commissioners recommended *some* alteration in the scale of these endowments, and, if I recollect rightly, they recommended that about one-tenth of the whole should be assigned to them.

"In 1870 a Royal Commission was appointed on *Scientific Instruction and the Advancement of Science*, presided over by the Duke of Devonshire, with Lubbock, Huxley, and other eminent men members of it. They made a report in 1875, recommending a much more prominent position to what they call the three 'non-classical' subjects —mathematics, modern languages, and natural science— to which they recommend that four-eighths of the time and importance should be assigned.

"Should you not have seen these reports, and wish to see them, I should be most pleased to send them. I should indeed be delighted to add the name of my fair cousin to the list of other illustrious advocates of reform.

"One word more. Assuming that the acquisition of a certain amount of knowledge of the ancient languages is desirable, do you think there is any doubt that they would be acquired with much less expenditure of time and feeling of drudgery at a later age than that ordinarily devoted to their acquisition? I will not detain you by discussing this point: suffice it to say that it seems probable that it would be so; and though our *present* system is so general as not to afford much opportunity of testing the question, experience has, I know, supported this view in the comparatively few instances where there has been the opportunity of testing it.

"I cannot help thinking that a certain halo surrounds the ancient languages by calling them the 'classics.' People are accustomed to attach the name classical to what is pure and refined in style in English composition, whether prose or poetry, and in the fine arts, including architecture,

and in every object of æsthetic feeling; and this term
they regard as the opposite to *vulgar.* And with a large
portion of the world there is some danger of their jumping
to the conclusion that the study of 'the classics' means
the formation of refined tastes in literature and the arts,
and is associated with the idea of refined social habits.
This is clearly a delusion, and if the use of the term
'classics' serves to perpetuate it, would it not be well to
substitute the term 'ancient languages'? The term
'classical' is most appropriate to the productions of higher
quality of the ancient as of the modern literature, but
surely not to those elementary studies which are now
commonly dignified with the name.

"Fortunately for you, my dear cousin, I sat down this
morning with the resolve that what I had to say should be
said within the limits of one day's morning hours, and I
will not consume more of your time by adding to my long
yarn of utterances another of apologies. I will only say
that the reform of our system of education has always
appeared to me to be of VITAL interest. *Some* improvement
there has been, no doubt, in our day, but its pace has been
very slow, and I long to see it accelerated. We all feel
it to be our duty to promote the reform of our political
institutions—to take out the crumbling walls and rotten
timbers, and to broaden and consolidate the foundations.

"This last and fundamental work we cannot, I think,
execute more effectually than by seeing to the foundations
that must be laid in early life.

"On looking over what I have said, I feel confirmed in

the misgivings I had on sitting down as to the prudence of handling so important a subject in this desultory manner, and I must ask you not to judge of the merits of the case by the feebleness of its advocacy.

"Do not think of troubling yourself to enter into a discussion with me. Just let this go for what it is worth. —Yours affectionately,

"F. SWANWICK."

But while in Mr. Swanwick's case the duties of the citizen were not forgotten in those of the professional man, so neither did his public duties in his retirement absorb and occupy all the powers of his rich social nature. Never was there a more thoughtful and devoted husband or parent.

The following recollections by his son, Mr. Russell Swanwick, of two excursions as a schoolboy with his father, present authentic illustrations of some of the beautiful aspects of Mr. Swanwick's character in his domestic relations :—

"I remember, as if it were but yesterday, two excursions which I enjoyed as a schoolboy with my father. The first of these comes vividly back to me like the most delightful of dreams. I was at school at Mr. Herford's, at Lancaster. In those days terms were twenty weeks instead of twelve, and my parents, thinking it a long absence for a little boy, my father most kindly came all the way down to Lancaster one fine October to take me for a two days' tour—all the *exeat* that was allowed in those days. Well do I remember that warmest and

D

heartiest of greetings; with all the home messages of love, and then the home news as we rushed along in the North express. The feeling was one of simply perfect happiness in that delightful warmth of sympathy. Then the maps were taken out and plans made for our little run to that enchanted region of the English Lakes, whose blue mountains I had seen away in the distance from the walks round Lancaster. The accounts I had heard from my father and mother of the ideal wedding tour they had taken on mountain ponies years before, had added a halo of delight to that lovely country. And now we were actually on our way there!

"As no train ran to Bowness that night, we had to be content with getting to the nearest point to the Lake district—Kendal. Tea was ordered at once, and then off to bed early, to be ready for the seven o'clock start the next morning for Bowness. We drove along Windermere, with occasional walks up the hills, and on to Keswick, where my recollection seems to land us at two or three o'clock. Then it was that my father divulged his plan, if it could be accomplished, of going up Skiddaw that evening. He knew the keen delight of a boy in a big mountain, and that too on pony back. So ponies and guide were immediately bespoken, while we were getting a hasty mouthful. As we rode up, the mountain became all crisp with frost, and higher still a sheet of ice, and the air became as clear as crystal, with the prospect of a most lovely sunset. And such it indeed was: all the Scotch mountains quite clear away to the north; the Isle of Man, with the distant coast of Ireland all visible; and the beautiful outlines of the nearer Lake mountains (which old friends my father pointed out) were all bathed in a most lovely sunset light. Oh, wasn't it cold! yet we felt nothing but the exhilaration, and ran and slid down to get ourselves warm. Then a truly Lake tea, a delightful chat by a warm fire, and early to bed, ready for another early start.

"Seven o'clock again, and a Sunday morning too, and I fancy all the more delightful for that reason, by contrast, to me certainly, perhaps to us both. And such a morning too! Everything white with frost—Keswick Lake a sheet of ice. What a ringing musical clatter the three horses' hoofs made on the hard road along the lake's side as we trotted gaily along; for we had each a horse, and one for the guide, as we had 27 miles to cover that day. I well recollect my father's delight at the foliage, for such wonderful autumn tints one seldom sees. (I think it was the recollection of this ride and the autumn colouring that led my father, some twenty years after, to take my mother and sister to see the Lakes in similar tints.) The day became delightfully warm as we got to Borrowdale, up which we rode, and then turned under the Langdale Pikes, and so to Ambleside, and then in the evening back to Lancaster. The worst was always the parting after such glimpses of perfect bliss. But my father always tried to impress on one the principle that the great advantage of pleasure was to come back refreshed for work, and left one morally toned to do one's best.

"The second of these excursions—a delightful two days

by Esthwaite Water and Coniston, and back by the foot of Windermere—was mainly a walking and boating excursion, very delightful, but not with such perfect weather, and it ended most eventfully. As we were travelling towards Lancaster by the fast mail train, and had, I think, both fallen asleep, a terrific series of bumps awoke us. A glance at my father showed me it was something serious, and he had only time to say, 'hold tight,' when the carriage heeled over and fell with a great crash on its side, and all was quiet! The intense feeling of relief was extraordinary. A young naval officer, who was in the carriage, climbed up and out of the window in no time, and, giving us a hand, we were soon out of the window, which lay upwards. We then helped those in the other compartments out. The scene in the bright moonlight was extraordinary. The whole train was strewn on either side of the embankment — a perfect wreck, and only three carriages, of which ours was one, lay on their sides on the top of the embankment. My father instantly went up the line to stop any approaching train, till the guard came and placed signals on the rails. We found that though most of the carriages were broken in pieces in their roll over, yet hardly any passenger was seriously hurt, and not one dangerously. Had we been upset a couple of hundred yards sooner, we should have been in a cutting, and the piling up of the carriages on one another would have been fearful; and had we been a little farther, we should have been on a high bridge. It was altogether, therefore, a most merciful escape. For years after, a sudden jerk of a train gave me an electric shock by no means agreeable, but my father's steadier nerves, and a thorough belief in the great work of his life, saved him from feeling any of these effects."

But the affectionateness of Mr. Swanwick's nature was marked as much by its breadth as its depth, so that a very large circle of friends enjoyed with his family a share in the wealth of his love. Never was there a man who took a keener delight in the society of his friends. It would be hardly possible to give any one who did not personally know him any just idea of the rich quality and the overflowing measures of the radiant and self-forgetful kindness with which it was his constant habit, to the very last, to brighten the lives of all who belonged to him by ties of kindred or friendship. Those who enjoyed the privilege of his friendship always found, as the occasion arose, that he could absolutely forget himself to promote their interests. He would freely give not only thought and time, but undergo great trouble and pain and vexation to do them service. And this would not be done under impulse, but after deep and careful consideration, with a steadiness which never wavered, and with that self-restraint which was characteristic of all his actions. Nor was he content to do his friends service for the moment; his care was to make it of permanent benefit.

Many men in Mr. Swanwick's circumstances and with his cultivated tastes would have been tempted on retiring from professional duties to remove into a neighbourhood at a greater distance from the yearly encroachments of the coal and iron industries. But his deep personal interest in the people amongst whom he had worked so long, and his strong sense of public duty, held him permanently to the spot which he had for many years made his home. And as a relative, a friend, and a neighbour, he made "Whittington" a name with an imperishable charm. Never was there a more delightful fireside than his, and to young and old alike he was the kindest and most charming of hosts. The same miraculous thoughtfulness which never let him forget a point in preparing the plans of a railway, caused him to anticipate every wish or want of each guest under his boundlessly hospitable roof. In his house you were under the care of the most watchful and inventive providence, and a providence always beaming with joy and intelligence. Old pupils remember and record his kindness to them in his busy professional days. His hospitality was even then unbounded and proverbial. The homesick pupil found under his roof a joyful and kindly welcome; and thus many a Sunday and holiday was cheered and brightened. And it is scarcely necessary to remark that a man of his character, and a man withal so competent in the business of life, necessarily exercised a deep and strong influence on the young men who were fortunate enough to enjoy his friendship. Touching evidence of this was given at his death. One who had thus been influenced (to give one instance from many) then referred to him as "the radiant source of so much happiness to others, whom I respected beyond all other men, whose advice I sought so often, and never in vain; but who was, most of all, a man whose simple presence killed every unworthy thought in those who had the privilege to be intimate with him."

And what the busy engineer loved to do, but for want of time could not do to the fulness of his heart, the retired gentleman revelled in with a delight and enthusiasm to the last such as but few can have beheld in the case of any other man. Christmas parties at Whittington! What happy scenes, what warmth of kindness, what brightness of delight, what glee amongst the young, and the dear host youngest and most gleeful of all! What blessed interludes were these in the midst of school-day banishment, or the hard grind of business! What happy memories do these Christmas and other holidays at Whittington call up in the minds of young and old who were privileged to share them! And who that was ever present at one of the excursions which Mr. Swanwick delighted to organize and direct from his home into the best scenery of Derbyshire, or to the Dukeries in Nottinghamshire, or to other favourite spots, can ever forget those red-letter days? On such occasions he delighted to gather into his large family party school-girls and school-boys, neighbouring ministers and clergymen,—in a word, any of his friends in whose invigoration and enjoyment he could make his own soul glad. What jovial and exhilarating drives they were, above all, to those who had the good fortune to share the front seat with their host! On such occasions he would never have a coachman, but kept up the good old institution of the postilion, and this long after the postboys were at all in practice.

In addition to the habitual large hospitality of his house, Mr. Swanwick made a point of using every opportunity which offered of entertaining distinguished representatives of literature and science, and particularly enlightened educationalists. It was on an occasion of this kind, to which reference was made above in another connection, that he invited George Stephenson, who was then residing at Chesterfield, to meet Emerson, who was on his first visit to England, and lecturing at Chesterfield. The meeting was a most interesting one, and in after years Mr. Swanwick furnished Mr. Smiles with the substance of the account of it which he adopted in his *Life of George Stephenson* :—

" In the spring of 1848, Mr. Stephenson was invited to Whittington House, near Chesterfield, the residence of his friend and pupil, Mr. Swanwick, to meet the distinguished American, Emerson.

" It was interesting to see those two remarkable men, so different in most respects, and whose lines of thought and action lay in such widely different directions, yet so quick to recognise each other's merits. Mr. Stephenson was not, of course, acquainted with Mr. Emerson as an author, and the contemplative American might not be supposed to be particularly interested beforehand in the English engineer, whom he knew by reputation only as a giant in the material world. But there was in both an equal aspiration after excellence, each in his own sphere,—the æsthetic and abstract tendencies of the one complementing the keen and accurate perceptions of the material of the other.

Upon being introduced, they did not immediately engage
in conversation; but presently Mr. Stephenson jumped up,
took Emerson by the collar, and, giving him one of his
friendly shakes, asked how it was that in England we
could always tell an American? This led to an interesting conversation, in the course of which Emerson said
how much he had everywhere been struck by the haleness
and comeliness of the English men and women; and this
diverged into a further discussion of the influences which
air, climate, moisture, soil, and other conditions exercised
upon the physical and moral development of a people.
From this the conversation was directed upon the subject
of electricity, upon which Mr. Stephenson launched out
enthusiastically, explaining his views by several simple and
striking illustrations. From thence it diverged into the
events of his own life, which he related in so graphic a
manner as completely to rivet the attention of the
American. Afterwards Emerson said 'that it was worth
crossing the Atlantic to have seen Stephenson alone; he
had such native force of character and vigour of intellect.' "

With reference to this interview it ought, however, to be
mentioned that Mr. Swanwick's *viva voce* description of it was
far more forcible and graphic than that which has been preserved in Mr. Smiles' interesting pages. Mr. Swanwick's
voice and manner rendered with peculiar vividness the different characters of his two eminent guests. He made you
feel George Stephenson's massive force, as in a step or two
he strode across the room, took his stand opposite Emerson,
seized him by the collar with both hands, and gave him a

friendly shake, as he asked, " What is it about you Americans that we can always tell you by ? "   He also made you realize Emerson's gentle, amused, and courteously admiring tone, as he responded, " Indeed, I cannot say.   There is something very pleasant to us in the aspect of an Englishman," or words to that effect.   It is also worth mentioning that it was after dinner when Stephenson opened out on the subject of electricity ; and, finding that the dining-room poker would not answer the purpose, and yet bent on his illustration not failing, he had the kitchen poker sent for, and with its help proceeded to expound his views.

This was almost the last occasion on which Mr. Swanwick met Stephenson.   It is needless to remark that he treasured the memory of his distinguished master, and delighted to recall incidents which illustrated the marked individuality and genius of the great man.   In his speech at the Stephenson Centenary at Chesterfield, June 9, 1881, he gave an interesting sketch of Stephenson's work as an engineer.   And it was interesting not only as an authentic description by one of Stephenson's colleagues of the great difficulties which had to be faced in the early days of railroad construction, but also as a record of the share Mr. Swanwick himself took in that great engineering enterprise.   With characteristic self-repression he did not, however, allude to his own doings at all, while he referred to the other members of the distinguished band,—Locke, Gooch, Allcard, and Dixon, in fitting terms of praise.[1]

As a rule, nine months of the year were thus spent by

[1] See Appendix C.

Mr. Swanwick at Whittington in the midst of public, domestic, and social duties. But, as has been observed previously, he was a genuine lover of both art and nature. In his busiest professional days he thoroughly enjoyed the beautiful scenery through which his business might take him, and he was then in the habit of snatching every possible opportunity of seeing also great works of architecture, painting, and statuary. His intensely social nature, however, made all such pleasures vastly greater when they could be enjoyed with friends. As soon, therefore, as he had got free from the trammels of his profession, and especially as soon as his son and daughter had reached an age at which they could share with their parents the advantages and delights of travel at home and abroad, he indulged more freely tastes which had always been naturally strong.

North Wales was a favourite resort, and there he purchased a small estate near Cader Idris in 1852, his sole indulgence in the luxury of landed property beyond his place at Whittington. It was in North Wales that he was once led, by his love of mountain fastnesses and his habitual determination not to be driven from his purpose, into an adventure which might have proved disastrous. He had set out by himself with the intention of ascending Cader Idris on the Dolgelly side, of crossing the summit, and of descending on the Towyn side. A boy was engaged as guide who was supposed to know the way across. But on reaching the summit Mr. Swanwick found that this supposed knowledge was purely imaginary. He accordingly sent the boy back by the route he had come, and, determined not to be beaten, and undeterred by the mist which was gathering, resolved to find his way by the aid of his ordnance map. The mist grew thicker, and, not being provided with a compass, his first attempt to reach the destination for which he had started landed him at the point from which he had set out. The afternoon was advancing, and in an hour or two darkness would add to the difficulties of the situation. Prompt and decided action was necessary. He resolved accordingly to walk in a straight line in the direction which he supposed was most likely the right one. At the same time he listened for the trickle of water, resolving not to leave it, however unpromising the track it took might seem. At length the welcome sound was heard, and it led to a streamlet which proved a rough but safe path. By dint of running and jumping he at last reached a point below the mist before the daylight was gone. After further walking under less rigorous conditions, he made his way to some cottages, where a guide was procured who enabled him to reach his destination.

As a rule, his love of nature was gratified after his retirement by a resort of some two months each year into the finer and wilder parts of the British isles. Few men knew more intimately, and few enjoyed with a keener relish, the beauties of English and Scotch scenery. By an annual visit with members of his family to London he combined the meeting of friends with the gratification of his artistic tastes.

In 1859, when his son and daughter had reached an age to profit by the opportunity, he gave himself and his family the treat of a ten months' sojourn on the Continent. This was the only prolonged stay abroad that he ever made. The tour included Paris, the Riviera, Rome, Naples, Paestum, and the towns of North Italy, the Italian Lakes, the Tyrol, Switzerland, and the Rhine. The beauty and grandeur of the scenery, and the pleasant characteristic features and habits of the people of the countries visited, remained probably the most prominent of the permanent recollections of the tour. In his case the relics of the past owed their chief interest to the force of the direct, sensible impression produced on the imagination, rather than to their antiquarian features. The ruined temples of Paestum, for instance, acquired much of their impressiveness for him from the wide malarious solitude which surrounds them, and where they had stood for two thousand years. And in Rome, though historical associations were by no means ignored, it was the actual existing grandeur of such monuments of the past as the Coliseum and other ruins, or of St. Peter's and other fine buildings, which so forcibly appealed to him. In the case of works of art no representation of human feeling in its higher, sweeter, and more spiritual forms failed to win his quick recognition, or to give him lively pleasure. On the other hand, he would always enter his protest against the tribute of admiration so frequently paid, wrongly as he conceived, on purely technical grounds. Mr. Russell Swanwick, recalling the tours he had taken with his father, remarks with regard to this one : " My father's deep interest in perfect pieces of architecture brought out in us a kindred interest, the source of which we hardly realized in those days. His eye for exact and beautiful curves in design was unusually keen, and made a deep impression on us. His distaste for the merely sensuously beautiful, without soul, in sculpture or painting, and his intense love of a truly good and beautiful face, both rise up amongst my fresh recollections of that delightful time amongst the works of the world's masters. The youth of both my father and my mother, and the energy and thoroughness with which they worked at all the sights of lasting interest, impresses one more and more as one grows older."

In the summer of 1865 Mr. Swanwick took his family again into Switzerland for three months; in 1869, to the Engadine; and in 1873 he accompanied his son to the Exhibition at Vienna. From Vienna he made a flying visit to the Semmering Railway, in which he took a deep professional interest as a piece of remarkable engineering; while the great beauty of the scenery through which this romantic line passes gave him keen delight. On the return home from Vienna, Mr. Swanwick and his son turned aside to see the finest parts of the Salzkammergut, with which he was greatly charmed.[1] Mr. Russell Swanwick's recollections of this tour incidentally record illustrations of some of those characteristics which made his father the most delightful of travelling companions :—

" The longest tour which I had the privilege of taking alone with him was on the occasion of the Vienna

[1] In Appendix F a few passages from letters written on these foreign tours to friends and members of his family are given, not as in any respect good specimens of his epistolary style, but as supplying indications of the objects of greatest interest to him as a traveller amidst foreign nations, the works of nature, and the creations of art.

Exhibition, when he most kindly agreed to accompany me, partly, I think, because I had not been very well before going, for he was not very fond of Exhibitions. The journey up the Rhine and down the Danube, with all the fine scenery on the latter, was most enjoyable. He was greatly pleased with the beautiful Valhalla near Regensburg, with the splendid view from the portico. Business detained me in Vienna longer than I expected, and kept us for some time away from the beautiful scenery. This was really a great denial to my father, but he most kindly refused to go off without me, though he was quite tired of his solitary walks in the Exhibition. Not by a word, however, did he express his wish to get away, as he would not hurry my business or make me feel I was keeping him. It was not till we were off in the train that he expressed what a delightful change he felt it to be out amongst the beautiful woods and hills. And most lovely scenery it was. The Salzkammergut was in its perfection. It was just the first burst of real summer weather, and we felt, after three weeks of penance, as if we were out on a holiday. Pouring rain greeted us on the steamer as we sailed down the Traunsee, and my father made me stand under shelter while he stood outside. Arrived at the end of the lake, nothing would have prevented his determined carrying out of our plan by driving twenty miles in wet things, had I not declared I was not up to it in such rain, that the hotel at Gmunden looked very delightful, and that it would be very nice to return by the steamer to it, and make a fair start the next morning.

My father's kind generosity in giving me the shelter and himself the wetting resulted in a slight chill that night, but a lovely warm morning the next day seemed to disperse the evil, and he magnanimously agreed that the beautiful drive on the lovely day rewarded us for turning back,—a proceeding I should think unknown to my father before. His favourite motto was, 'Fortune favours the brave,' and many an excursion does one recollect when the weather which looked impossible turned out delightfully beautiful. The scenery about Ischl was lovely, and never was my father more delighted with anything than with the Koenigsee. Many a time did he long to transport my mother and sister over to enjoy it with us. Whenever he greatly enjoyed anything, his first thought was to share it with others. We spent a day amongst the splendid paintings in Munich, and then came back by express train to England; and so ended our tour, full of so many delightful memories."

With the exception of these few continental tours, the annual excursions into the finer parts of the British isles and an annual visit to London formed the principal change from his customary life at Whittington with his family, amongst his friends, and in the midst of regular public duties. He kept himself fully posted up in current politics and the more important social questions of the day, above all in the progress of education. The newspapers and political periodicals of importance he read regularly, mastering the facts and arguments of real weight on subjects of special interest to him. Books of modern history and travel were his favourite reading.

When guests were not staying in his house, or, if so, when it was equally pleasant to them, the reading aloud in the evening of books of this description was a great enjoyment to him. In these and other ways he kept up a keen and intelligent interest in the history and progress of his country and fellow-men.

This sketch of Mr. Swanwick's life and character, slight as it is, must not omit a reference to the attitude of his mind towards religion. He belonged, as we have seen, by his descent and education, to that body of dissenters which is commonly known by the name of Unitarians. By choice and personal conviction, he remained throughout his life an earnest adherent of this religious community. Its ministers were amongst his dear and intimate friends, and not a few of them hold his memory in deep and grateful veneration. To the congregation of this body meeting in the Elder Yard Chapel, Chesterfield, with which he was personally connected from first coming into the neighbourhood, he was a most generous friend. But he did not regard the growth of his own or any other religious community as the main hope of human progress. For this he looked rather to the school than to the church. Anything approaching ecclesiastical or clerical assumption or intolerance was inexpressibly abhorrent to his nature, and he would undoubtedly have declined to be classed as a Unitarian, if the name was meant to signify the profession of a creed or adherence to an ecclesiastical party, and not loyalty to religious enlightenment, freedom, equality, and progress. Believing sincerely that his church stood

E

for these great human interests, he was always ready, when important occasions called for his help, to contribute largely of his time and substance in promoting and defending its true principles. For instance, he took deep interest in the important fight between the old and the new school of Unitarians, which ended in favour of the latter, by their triumph at a great meeting in Manchester in 1857, which he attended. A formidable protest had been made on the part of the representatives of the old school against the appointment of Dr. Martineau (then the Rev. James Martineau) and the Rev. J. J. Taylor to the professorships of Manchester New College on its removal from Manchester to London. Martineau particularly was charged with marked tendencies to infidelity, and a virtual betrayal of positive or historical Christianity. The protest was largely signed, and the professors felt that they could not retain their posts without some decisive expression of confidence from the great body of the trustees of the college. By the constitution of his mind, the habit of his life, and the principles of his thinking, Mr. Swanwick could take but little immediate interest in the theological aspects of the question at issue, but he held tenaciously and enthusiastically by the principles of free inquiry, free teaching, and progress; and on this ground gave his vote and support most earnestly to the professors. In after-life he often referred with satisfaction to the triumph of the principle of free inquiry on that occasion, and always spoke with greatest admiration of the ability with which the Rev. J. H. Thom led the glorious fray in defence of liberty. In the congregation at Chesterfield he was the staunch ally of any minister who thought and spoke freely, to the alarm at times of orthodox Unitarians.

I have said that he was, by his mental constitution and the habit of his life, disinclined to meddle with purely theological questions. His mind was pre-eminently practical, with a decided predisposition unfavourable to theoretical speculation. Indeed, apart from theology, he was not in the least degree a speculative philosopher. His religion was consequently mainly ethical. To do the will of God in the service of man, not to know the Divine nature or the Divine purposes, was the ruling desire of his life. But conscientious devotion to every private and public obligation was in his case attended by the deep feeling, the humble submission, the firm faith, and the cheering hope which constitute the essence of religion as distinguished from theological representations of it.

And here one cannot but recall the description in the New Testament of "pure religion and undefiled before God." No account of Mr. Swanwick's character, life, or religion may pass unnoticed his constant, sympathetic, and delicate attention to his friends in trouble, sorrow, need, sickness, or any other adversity. The constancy, the inventiveness, the tenderness, and the unobtrusiveness of his overflowing kindness was, under all circumstances, most marked; and when the finest chords of his intensely sympathetic nature were touched by any calamity which might have befallen his friends, nothing could be more

beautiful than the expression then evoked of these fine qualities of his kindness. He was master, almost without a rival, of the art of making himself appear the person under obligation when he had done a kind act, and he excelled himself even when he ministered in any way to others in their trials. Amongst the touching expressions of grateful affection which his death called forth, there is one from Miss Hutton, his cousin, the very old friend of his youth referred to above, which may be given as an illustration of his kindness in such circumstances. Speaking of a time when she was approaching her seventieth year, she says :—"The next visit he made was after my dear mother's death, when I was quite, quite lonely, having lost both my parents. He most kindly insisted on my accompanying him to his house in Wales, where I was truly happy. He gave me delightful drives in Wales, and did everything to make me happy." Of the younger generation another wrote at the same time :—"Through the sorrow came flooding over me innumerable recollections of happy days . . . of perpetual kindnesses received, and of help given to my life by his bright example." Another :—
"There are so many outside your own family circle, who, like myself, will remember him not only as a kind friend, but as one of the few whose pure characters and Christian lives help to make their fellows better."

We have now come to the end of this bright and useful life. In the autumn of 1884, signs of failing health began to show themselves. And as he had his life through enjoyed a rare immunity from sickness and weakness, his friends, and he himself, continued for a long time to hope that the vigour of his constitution would overcome the debility which the medical men could not trace to any organic disease. But the hope was not fulfilled. By the autumn of the next year his strength was greatly reduced. A stay of some weeks in Gloucestershire, in the fine air of the Cotswolds, to which the neighbourhood of his son's residence formed an additional attraction, failed to work any change for the better. The sea was next tried, and he removed to Bournemouth; but still no improvement resulted. Before he left home in the late summer, he had put all his affairs in characteristically perfect order, as though he had antici-pated the end. But he kept up to the last his deep interest in the affairs of his friends and his country. It was also a relief and pleasure to him to have his youngest grandchildren brought into his room. At length, November 15, 1885, he passed from the loving ministrations of his wife and children into the keeping of that Divine Love, of which he had been, through his life, a faithful servant and devout worshipper.

His mortal remains were brought home to Whittington,[1] and on 21st November laid in the cemetery at Chesterfield, amid expressions of profound regard and esteem from far and near, from all ranks and parties.

> " Sweet day ! so cool, so calm, so bright,
>   Bridal of earth and sky ;
> The dew shall weep thy fall to-night,
>   For thou, alas ! must die.

[1] See Appendix G.

Sweet rose ! in air whose odours wave,
  And colour charms the eye ;
Thy root is ever in its grave,
  And thou, alas ! must die.

Sweet spring ! of days and roses made,
  Whose charms for beauty vie ;
Thy days depart, thy roses fade,
  Thou too, alas ! must die.

Only a sweet and holy soul
  Hath tints that never fly ;
While flowers decay and seasons roll,
  It lives, and cannot die !"

One Sunday, in the Elder Yard Chapel, Chesterfield, when this hymn of George Herbert's had been sung at the close of the morning service, he said to me, as we were leaving the chapel, with evident feeling, " What a beautiful hymn the last was !" The remark and the tone of it made a deep impression upon me, for I could not help regarding the hymn as not only representing his faith in the immortality of goodness, but as describing the sweetness and tenderness of his nature.

APPENDIXES.

APPENDIX A.

Diary of the Construction of Grosvenor Bridge, June 1827
to June 1828.

THERE exists in manuscript, in Frederick Swanwick's neat
and clear handwriting of that period, a full and careful
diary of the progress of the construction of the Grosvenor
Bridge, from 12th June 1827 to June 1828. The diary
is illustrated by minute pen drawings of the work—the
dams, pumps, pile-engines, rams, various other tools and
engines, and the different stages of the undertaking.
Every instrument and operation is described with the
minuteness and clearness characteristic of the working of
a mind which could not rest until every point had been
seen through in all its details and bearings. Even the
financial aspects of the operations are carefully noted.
The difficulties of the work are described with all the
interest of a love of battling with them. Even a lay
reader of it must feel that it amply sustains the prophecy
of Mr. Thomas Wicksteed (see *ante*, p. 8), based on a
letter written at the same period.

APPENDIX B.

Letters from George Stephenson.

ALTON GRANGE, *September 29th*, 1834.

DEAR SWANWICK,—I have this evening received yours of September 25th. The contents of your letter are very satisfactory. I should advise you not to spend too much money in surveying and levelling until you see the York and Leeds Line get under weigh. I have not heard from the York people since I left. I imagine they are waiting until after the meeting of the Corporation. It is quite out of the question to expect that the Great North Line will go on for many years to come, therefore little regard ought to be paid to it in setting out the line. My view is that the shortest line from Pickering to York ought to be made first; and also the best line from York to Leeds. The low line which was talked of at the York meeting as being the best to join the Great North Line is quite out of the question in my opinion, as it would put an extra tonnage on all goods coming from Leeds to York, Malton, Pickering, and Whitby. You will have, I have no doubt, time to finish your Whitby work before you are wanted at York, if they only let us have a beginning at it. I have no doubt we shall get them to let us go to Parliament. I am determined to push the line to Loughboro'. I may probably want your assistance in that, if the York should not go on. You may just do as you like about my name appearing in the advertisement for tenders, but if you like to have your own name in, do so.—Yours truly,　　　GEORGE STEPHENSON.

P.S.—Mr. ——'s statement to the York people is certainly a most shameful one with respect to the horse-power. If he had wished to make a fair statement, he should have brought the locomotive speed down to the horse speed, and then considered the cost. Taking locomotive engines at twenty miles per hour, and horses at ten, locomotives will be four times as cheap. At three miles an hour, locomotives are about one-half cheaper. The higher the power, the more does the locomotive gain on the horses. G. S.

NEW TUN, DERBY, *October 18th,* 1835.

DEAR SWANWICK,—The people in this country appear to be going mad altogether in railway schemes. I have written to the Huddersfield solicitors, recommending them to apply to you to examine and lay out the line, which I think you would soon do, and set some surveyors to work to prepare the plans and sections. I have had a letter from Brackenbury of Manchester, requesting me to meet the Committee of the Manchester and Leeds Railway as soon as possible. I have, however, thrown a good deal of cold water on that scheme, as the prospects of it are very much altered since the projection of the North Midland Railway.

I have, however, promised to meet them in the course of a fortnight, and they can give the notices if they like.

I have also had another letter from the Pottery gentlemen requiring more information. I have not yet received any letter from the York people, which I had expected.   I should not like that part of the line to fall into any other hands than ours.

If you wish to write to me on any subject, I expect to be home on Wednesday, after which I shall set off to London.   Direct to the Albion.   To-morrow I shall be at Belper.—Yours truly,   GEORGE STEPHENSON.

F. SWANWICK, Esq.

P.S.—The shares for the Birmingham and Derby Line will be all filled up by the end of this week.   I have been over the whole line.   It is one continued flat almost from end to end.

APPENDIX C.

Speech at the Centenary of George Stephenson's birth, June 9, 1881, celebrated at Chesterfield, as reported in the " Derbyshire Courier."

Mr. Swanwick, who on rising was received with loud cheers, said: Before proposing the toast which had been entrusted to him, they would perhaps allow him to break in somewhat upon the course prescribed.   After the eloquent and feeling references of their noble chairman to the subject of their meeting to-day—the great engineer, George Stephenson—he felt that as one of his early friends, and as one who lived with him for many years, it would be contrary to his instincts to remain silent and not to make some remarks in support of the admirable speech that had been delivered. It was probably not given to many gentlemen present to pay the tribute of respect to the memory of George Stephenson by attending when his remains were conveyed to the tomb; unfortunately it was not his privilege to be present. He was travelling in a distant part of the country when he heard of the death of his old master. He had not even heard of his illness. They could well understand how great was the shock to him when he heard that the man whom he had venerated—and who was worthy to be venerated—had passed from amongst them. He needed scarcely to say that he posted home with the utmost possible speed, but he was too late to join in showing his respect by his attendance at the funeral of the great engineer. He would not, however, dwell upon that. He apprehended that they were come there to rejoice in the birth and in the life of George Stephenson. It would be an impertinence on his part to dwell upon the life in detail, as it had been so admirably written by Mr. Smiles in what was known as *The Life of George Stephenson.* After strongly recommending all to read the work, he said he was happy to see that Mr. Smiles or his publishers had wisely published a centenary edition of the *Life of George Stephenson,* at a very cheap rate. Although he might not be entitled to occupy their time by referring to the details of the life so admirably written by Mr. Smiles, yet, having been intimately acquainted personally with the subject of their meeting, he could not forbear from giving them a few touches or incidents illustrative of his experience and knowledge of the great engineer. He became acquainted with Mr. Stephenson as a pupil while the Liverpool Railway was in progress, and he was therefore a witness of all the enormous labour he had to undergo in the accomplishment of that work. They must recollect that engineering was not then as it is now. The position of the engineer now was simply to lay out a line; to make drawings and specifications for the work; and then to call upon some experienced contractor to undertake the execution of it—it might be ten, twenty, fifty, or one hundred miles in length. That was the duty of the engineer now. But in the days of the Liverpool and Manchester Railway, Mr. Stephenson used to leave his house before breakfast in the morning, and visit the works not far from his house. There he used to employ his hours in designing every detail of the work. He had to design the waggons that were to move the earth, and the cranks that were to lift the stone. The implements that were to lay the permanent way he had to design, and direct every detail of the great work. Therefore they would see he had much work to do of which they had no idea in these days; and that was how George Stephenson spent the early part of the day. After a hasty breakfast, and having given directions to his resident pupils and others, he would mount his favourite horse Bobby and visit the works, or, it may be, mount his gig and visit the works on different parts of the line; for he never travelled except in the simplest way. He would return late in the evening to a hasty dinner; but the work of the day was not then over with him. He had then to dictate his letters; give instructions for the transaction of business, and the forwarding of works on the following day or the next week. All this had to be done; this was his measure of work, and was not completed perhaps until nine or ten o'clock at night. George Stephenson would then in the strength of his simplicity indulge in some unbending. He would then to his pupils and his friends relate incidents that had occurred in his early life; and those incidents which impressed him most, and which he was fondest of recording, were those which referred to his hardest work, and to the uphill life he had led. He would also refer with great and honest and just pride to the great work he effected in early life—the invention of the safety lamp. That was absolutely his invention. There was no doubt about that; and they would find the evidence for it was ample and complete. If there were wanting any confirmation of it, it was found in the fact that the railway proprietors, thinking that he was more immediately connected with it, presented him, amongst other gifts, with the handsome donation of £1000. They would recognise in that fact that there was an entire recognition on their part of the completeness of the discovery. At these evening gatherings, Mr. Stephenson indulged in a fine play of humour—or, in other terms, in "chaffing his pupils." He would remark upon the lazy habits of the present generation, and say, "You don't know what wark is. You know nothing about wark. You should have lived in my early life, then you would have seen what wark really was." He also knew what work was in his manhood. It was quite unnecessary that he should speak in detail of the enormous work of constructing the Liverpool and Manchester Railway. They knew how the great engineer smoothed over the difficulties connected with Chat Moss, and accomplished the work. No doubt there were works now of greater magnitude in connection with railways and other undertakings in other parts of the kingdom, but these had been made since the days of the Liverpool and Manchester Railway. In those days the work was regarded as one of the most stupendous character, and they must recollect that the great engineer had no competent assistants. What he (the speaker) meant was, that although he had very able men associated with him, they were, like himself, almost inexperienced. They had to feel their own way in the accomplishing of their great works; and most ably did they aid their master in the performance of their duties. Perhaps it was scarcely necessary to refer to men like Locke and Gooch, and Allcard and Dixon, who were his four principal assistants in the execution of the Liverpool and Manchester Railway. They performed their duties as readily and with as much vigour as could be expected of them, and as worthy of the master under whom they acted. But there came a more important period in the history of the great engineer. His great work approached completion, and it had to be decided what should be the tractive power on the railway; whether horses or fixed engines or locomotive engines. Mr. Stephenson having had experience of the construction of locomotive engines, felt strongly that locomotive power should be the power employed; but there was a strong protest made against the employment of locomotive power.

There were those who asserted that the locomotive engine in the north had not proved itself equal to meeting the condition of safety, and therefore the public mind was not prepared to give its verdict in favour of the locomotive system. Some of the most influential directors of the Liverpool and Manchester Railway were decidedly opposed to the introduction of the locomotive engine; and when in the progress of the work it became necessary to remove a vast amount of earth-work, the order was given that horses should be employed in its removal. This was a great annoyance, they might be sure, to the eminent engineer, but he persevered, and when he again brought the matter under the consideration of the directors they said they were not yet prepared to adopt the locomotive engine. Then they called upon two eminent engineers to report upon the matter. They visited the collieries in the north, and the Stockton and Darlington Railway, and they reported in favour of a system of fixed engines. They prepared an elaborate report, which looked extremely well on paper, showing that the line should be worked by, he thought, about twenty fixed engines placed along the line of the Liverpool and Manchester Railway. The scheme seemed extremely feasible, but it was contrary to the convictions of the great engineer. He said, "No; this system will never answer, and I will never abandon my favourite project of a locomotive engine;" and then it was that he called in the assistance of his son and one or two of his senior pupils, Locke and Gooch, to assist him in reporting on the report. It was a time of great anxiety to him, for he felt that the question of the locomotive engine hung in the balance, and it was all but determined that the fixed system should be adopted, but it was proposed as a *dernier ressort* that a premium should be offered for the best engine which could fulfil the conditions of safety and speed. The trial of the claims of that engine was witnessed by crowds of people from Liverpool and Manchester, and the "Rocket" not only fulfilled all the conditions that had been prescribed by the judges, but more than those conditions. Instead of running at a rate of eight or ten miles per hour, it was found to be capable of running at a speed of thirty miles per hour. The success of the "Rocket" established at once and for ever the system of the locomotive engine. He wished to say distinctly and deliberately, that if it had not been for the determined resolution of George Stephenson—if it had not been for that man applying the full powers of his mind and the energies of his body to the one object of overcoming all the difficulties which were presented in opposition to the use of the locomotive engine—England would have been saddled with a system of fixed engines on the Liverpool and Manchester Railway. If once that system had been introduced, and a large amount of capital had been invested in that system, it would have been necessary to go on trying to cobble it up and improve it, and to try and make it work. So they might have gone on for years trying to make it work, and the effect would have been that the system of railways, not merely during the remainder of the life of George Stephenson, but for tens of years, or a longer period, would have been worked by a system of fixed engines. George Stephenson not only exercised his usual force of judgment, but he did more than that, he exercised a moral courage in the face of difficulties under which many men would have quailed, when he was opposed by the directors of the Liverpool and Manchester Railway, and treated almost with contumely. He showed a moral courage which few could manifest, in order to achieve the victory he did achieve, and he felt it strongly—as his lordship [Lord Edward Cavendish] had said—that England and the world at large owed to Stephenson a debt of gratitude which could not be exaggerated. He thought he had occupied the time of the meeting longer than he ought to have done, but at the same time he felt that a matter of such intense interest to himself personally, and, as he thought, of such interest to the world at large, should not go without some record from one who was at least personally acquainted with all the details of the contest. Almost the last occasion upon which he had the satisfaction of being with Stephenson was when, as his guest, he met with the celebrated American thinker and literary man, Emerson, and upon that occasion (it seemed almost prophetic in these days, when magnetism and electricity in all its forms was seen to be having such sway in the world) the conversation was occupied almost entirely by the theory on these subjects expounded by Stephenson, the American sitting by and drinking it all in. It seemed almost prophetic that in the last few hours of his existence, Stephenson should have been propounding the theory that magnetism

and electricity were becoming, and would become, great powers
in the world.   He believed that prophecy—if prophecy he
might call it—would ultimately become true.   He was
sorry he had detained them so long from the toast which
had been placed in his hands, and which he could have
wished had been placed in more worthy hands—it was
the toast of " The Lord Bishop and Clergy of the Diocese
and Ministers of all Religious Denominations."

APPENDIX D.

*Note on Mr. Swanwick's Professional Work, contributed by
    Mr. Arnold Lupton, M.I.C.E., F.G.S., of the Yorkshire
    College, Leeds.*

Though no complete professional diary of Mr. Swanwick's
exists, a few contemporary memoranda, drawings, and
other papers give indications of some of the work which
fell to his hand.   The greater part of it was done in
association with George or Robert Stephenson, they leaving
the execution of it almost entirely to him, being themselves engaged in other enterprises absorbing their time.

The following tabular statement may be interesting as
showing some of the railway work which Mr. Swanwick
undertook in those years of his professional labours of
which any records remain amongst his papers.[1]   (It must

---

[1] The railways were surveyed in the autumn of one year, and submitted
to Parliament the spring and summer of the succeeding year, hence two
dates are given for each line, as 1845-6.

be noted that with regard to all the railways named where Mr. Swanwick was assistant engineer, he received his appointment from the Company, to whom he was responsible, upon Mr. Stephenson's recommendation.)

1832.   *Whitby and Pickering Railway*, 24 miles—George Stephenson, engineer. Mr. Swanwick surveyed the country entirely himself, and, after a joint-inspection of it with Mr. Stephenson, laid out the line, designed and specified the works, and superintended the construction.

1833.   *Whitby and Pickering Railway.* Making drawings and superintending works.
Assisting Mr. Stephenson in his railway work in Leicestershire, Staffordshire, Cheshire, and Lancashire.

1834–5.   *Whitby and Pickering Railway.* Construction.
Midland and East Junction Railway—George Stephenson, engineer-in-chief; Frederick Swanwick, assistant engineer. Mr. Swanwick surveyed this railway.
Stockport and Warrington Railway — George Stephenson, engineer-in-chief; Frederick Swanwick, assistant engineer. Mr. Swanwick surveyed this line, and made estimates and reports.
Assisting Mr. Stephenson in his railway work in Leicestershire, Staffordshire, Cheshire, and Lancashire.

1835–6.   *Whitby and Pickering Railway.* Construction.
Stockport and Manchester Railway, 7 miles—George Stephenson, chief engineer; Frederick Swanwick, assistant engineer. Superintended survey, Parliamentary plans and sections, borings to prove ground, detailed estimates, gave evidence in Committee of Parliament.
Manchester and South Union Railway, 71 miles. Examined the country, and attended in London to oppose other railways.
Huddersfield and Leeds Railway, 16 miles—George Stephenson, engineer-in-chief; Frederick Swanwick, assistant engineer. Examined the country, superintended surveys, set out the line, made plans and sections for deposit with Clerks of the Peace, made drawings of works, estimates of cost.
London and Blackwall Railway. Consulted about this.
York and North Midland Railway, 20 miles—George Stephenson, consulting engineer; Frederick Swanwick, assistant engineer. Examined the country, superintended the

survey and deposit of plans, *made duplicate plans*, detailed drawings of bridges, detailed estimate, superintended valuation of land, canvassed landowners, attended Committees of Parliament.

North Midland Railway, 72 miles — George Stephenson, engineer-in-chief ; Frederick Swanwick, assistant engineer. Examined country from Derby to Leeds, superintended surveys, made drawings, detailed estimates, attended Committees of Parliament.

Sheffield and Rotherham Railway, 5 miles—Frederick Swanwick, engineer. Examined country, superintended surveys, deposited plans, made drawings, estimates, attended Parliamentary Committees.

1836–7. *Whitby and Pickering Railway.* Completed construction.

North Midland Railway. Setting out railway, making detailed drawings, letting contracts, superintending construction.

Doncaster, North Midland, and Goole Railway, 22 miles— Frederick Swanwick, acting engineer. Superintended surveys, examined the country, waited upon landowners, made estimates.

1838–40. *North Midland Railway.* Constructing and completing.

Sheffield and Rotherham Railway. Constructing and completing.

No notes of other work discovered, but it is most probable that he had other work.

1841–4. *North Midland Railway.* Resident engineer.

No notes of special work, but probably engaged in projecting, surveying, depositing plans, obtaining Acts of Parliament for extensions of the Midland Railway, such as the Erewash Valley Railway, Nottingham and Lincoln, Nottingham and Mansfield, Pinxton and Mansfield, Junction Railways between Midland Railway and Manchester, Sheffield, and Lincolnshire—about 80 miles of railway ; also numerous branch railways to collieries (say 10 miles). Mr. Swanwick was the engineer for all these railways.

1844–5. *Darfield to Worsborough*, 5 miles ; *Darfield to Elsecar*, 3 miles ; *Cheret to Horbury*, 4 miles ; *Oakenshaw to Wakefield*, 3 miles ; *Ambergate to Crich*, 3 miles—Robert Stephenson and Frederick Swanwick, engineers. Country examined, lines surveyed, plans deposited, estimates and designs made.

Swinton to Lincoln Railway, 44 miles—Robert Stephenson and Frederick Swanwick, engineers. Examined country, superintended survey, deposited plans, made estimates and designs. Attending Committees of Parliament, and opposing Wakefield, Pontefract, and Goole Railways, also Manchester, Sheffield, and Midland Junction Railway.

1845-6. *Leeds, Wakefield, and Midland Junction Railway*, 6 miles—Frederick Swanwick, engineer. Examined country, took trial levels, superintended surveys, lithograph plans and sections, attended Parliamentary Committees.

Great Grimsby, Louth, Horncastle, Lincoln, and Midland Junction Railway, say 45 miles — Frederick Swanwick, engineer. Examined country, superintended surveys, deposited plans, made drawings, estimates, examined opposing railway projects, attended Committees of Parliament.

Eastern Counties Railway, 54 miles—Robert Stephenson and Frederick Swanwick, engineers. Examined country, directing and completing surveys, detailed estimates, attended Parliamentary Committees.

Sheffield, Bakewell, and West Midland Railway, 35 miles—George Stephenson and Frederick Swanwick, engineers.

Northampton, Banbury, and Cheltenham Railway. Offered appointment as engineer.

Darfield to Worsborough, 5 miles; *Darfield to Elsecar*, 3 miles; *Chevet to Horbury*, 4 miles—Robert Stephenson and Frederick Swanwick, engineers. Second application to Parliament.

Swinton to Lincoln. Robert Stephenson and Frederick Swanwick, engineers. Second application to Parliament.

Lincoln to South Milford, 53 miles—Robert Stephenson and Frederick Swanwick, engineers. Examined the country, superintended surveys, deposited plans, made drawings and estimates.

1846-7. *Sheffield, Barnsley, Doncaster, and Goole Railway*, 43 miles—Robert Stephenson and Frederick Swanwick, engineers. Examined country, superintended surveys, deposited plans, made drawings and estimates.

Shropshire Union Railway, 55 miles—Robert Stephenson and Frederick Swanwick, engineers. Examined country, superintended surveys, deposited plans, made drawings and estimates.

Wakefield and Harrogate Railway, 18 miles — Frederick Swanwick, engineer. Examined country, superintended surveys, deposited plans, made drawings and estimates.

1847-8. *Newark and Gainsboro' Railway*, 20 miles—Robert Stephenson and Frederick Swanwick, engineers. Superintended surveys, deposited plans, made drawings and estimates.

1848-50. No notes of any new enterprises, was engaged completing Midland Railway Branches already authorized, such as Nottingham and Mansfield, opened in 1848; Midland and Sheffield and Manchester, opened in 1847; Erewash Valley, completed in 1848; Nottingham and Lincoln; many branch railways in Midland system.

Roughly speaking, this table shows that Mr. Swanwick surveyed about 600 miles of railway, of which he constructed himself about 200 miles; of the remaining 400 a considerable length has been constructed by other engineers. If there was a complete record, it would probably contain a considerably increased mileage of railways.

The above simple statement gives to the engineer the impression of great and sustained effort, but by others it should be read in the light of the following extract from a diary made by Mr. Swanwick, and which gives a fair sample of the way in which his time was occupied:—

" On Thursday (23rd October 1835) went over the line (projected North Midland Railway) on foot to Darfield, and returned to Wakefield; on Friday I saw Sir E. D——. I went on to Sheffield the next evening; and on Saturday, 25th October, I saw Mr. V——, and met him at Rotherham as to the Sheffield and Rotherham Line. On the same evening Mr. H—— called upon me at the Tontine, Sheffield. On Sunday I went over the Dronfield Line with G—— (an assistant), and walked back on the North Midland from Chesterfield to Rotherham (sixteen miles). On Monday morning I went over with B—— (an assistant) to Wakefield, where I met a deputation from the Committee of the Huddersfield and Leeds Railway, and was engaged as their engineer. On Tuesday morning I rode over the line to Huddersfield, and returned to Wakefield the same day. In the afternoon I went over the line of the York and North Midland Railway. I met some of the Committee (of the projected Railway Company) the same evening. On Wednesday I rode over the line to Fairburn, and met the Committee in the evening. I returned to Wakefield the same evening, and went on to Sheffield on Thursday morning; I there met the Sheffield Committee of the North Midland Railway, and presented a section of the Dronfield Line. The same day I met the Committee of the Sheffield and Rotherham Railway. On Friday I met a deputation of the Committee of the Sheffield and Rotherham at Rotherham. On Saturday morning I went with Mr. Stephenson to Sir G. Sitwell's (a large landowner on the North Midland), and thence to Barnsley. On Sunday, 2nd November, we went back to Darfield, and thence to Wakefield, where we saw Mr. M———. We went on the same day to Tadcaster, and the following morning to York, and back to Wakefield. We went on the same day to Huddersfield, and the following morning to Manchester, where I saw Mr. G——— and Mr. B———. The same evening (Tuesday, 4th November) I went over to Stockport, saw Mr. V———. The following day I walked over the line with the Committee, and returned *via* Huddersfield to Wakefield the same evening."

In the speech given in the Appendix C., Mr. Swanwick

described the difficulties of a railway engineer sixty years ago, in the person of George Stephenson. What was true of Stephenson was, to some extent, true of Mr. Swanwick. Though he benefited by the experience already gained in the construction of the first railways, still they were a new thing, and required from the engineer a great deal of original thought and contrivance. And the methods of work then devised have been but little altered up to the present date.

First, the engineer rides or walks (Mr. Swanwick generally walked when time permitted) over the country to examine it, marking on some small map the route that seems most feasible. Then he takes the trial levels, or sends his surveyors to do it, by means of which he discovers the relative altitudes of places on the route, and is enabled to mark out the best and cheapest railway. In choosing the route, the faculty which Mr. Swanwick possessed of ready mental calculation served him well; he was able to estimate approximately the cost of all the necessary works for alternative routes, and decide on the best, that did not exceed the amount that he thought it reasonable to spend. It may be noted that all the railways actually constructed by Mr Swanwick were made for a very moderate cost in comparison with their importance; hence they have in many cases been exceedingly profitable lines. The leading features of these lines are, that they traverse fertile country and connect important towns, that they follow the course of the valleys, so that good gradients and curves of large radius are obtained without heavy works in the shape of deep cuttings and high viaducts. Good gradients, that is to say, inclines not steeper than 1 in 260 (the worst gradient on the North Midland), were then considered essential for a locomotive railway; when steeper gradients (such as 1 in 80) were necessary, an additional engine was used to help the trains up the hill. This was owing to the small size of the first locomotives, which made them incapable of drawing a considerable train uphill. With the improvement of locomotives, the engineer has a greater choice of routes, because trains can now ascend gradients of 1 in 100 with ease, and 1 in 30 with difficulty. Next in importance to good gradients come good curves, which permit a very rapid traffic to be carried on with safety. Mr. Swanwick combined good gradients and good curves with economy in construction.

But to continue with the work of the engineer. Having selected the route, he directs the survey of a plan and the levelling of a section to be presented to Parliament, a work requiring the utmost care and accuracy, as a trifling error in the levels would probably result in the defeat of the project. Here Mr. Swanwick's untiring and conscientious care earned for him the reputation of an engineer who never failed. Then he had to prepare detailed designs and estimates, and state all the facts before a Parliamentary Committee. It was his habit to go over the ground himself before giving evidence, so that he was always completely informed before he entered the witness-box. After Parliament has sanctioned the railway, then follow fresh surveys, plans and sections on a large scale for the guidance of workmen, detailed drawings and specifications, the selection of contractors, the superintendence of the work. It has been said that genius is the faculty of taking infinite pains. Mr. Swanwick exhibited this faculty in many ways,—just going to look for himself to see if the work was properly done; never satisfied with anything less than the best possible design; selecting every stone quarry of which the produce might be used for his bridges; making in his note-book a sketch of any new or good design that caught his attention.

APPENDIX E.

Speech at Whittington at the Election of 1868, *as reported in the " Derbyshire Courier."*

The Chairman, in opening the business, said : Brother electors, I need scarcely tell you for what purpose we are assembled here to-day. It is to receive two honourable gentlemen who have put themselves in the van to represent this district of East Derbyshire. I need not tell you what an onerous duty that is, and how greatly indebted we are to them for sacrificing their pleasure and acquaintances in these dog-days of July, in order to give us all the information they can, and all you can ask as to the principles on which they propose to represent us in Parliament. It will not be necessary, in fact it would be indecorous, if I were to refer personally to Captain Egerton and Mr. Strutt. They are before you, and they will speak of their own views on the questions which are interesting to the public, and it would scarcely be good taste that I should refer to them, inasmuch as they will expound their own political opinions. But seeing that we are assembled within twenty yards of the Revolution House in which the Revolution of 1688 was planned, and when we remember that the Earl of Devonshire was an active agent in the consultation that then took place, and which ended in inviting the Prince of Orange to take the place of that bigoted and stupid, for such he was, King James, who thought he could rule, not by the voice of his people, but by what he called the right-divine—when I say we recollect we are in close proximity to that place, I feel that we are strictly on classic ground, and we would not ignore that fact, especially when we have present as one of our candidates a gentleman intimately connected with the family of Devonshire — a family which has since the completion of the Revolution stood firm to the principles which were then advocated, and which have tended to so much improve the fabric of the constitution. And now, prepared as most of that family are, Mr. Egerton is also prepared to assist in giving one finishing stroke to that fabric by asserting the opinion of nearly every subject of this realm before their country and their God as to the injustice done to a particular branch of this empire. I need scarcely say I allude to the Irish people. A fine, large-hearted, and chivalrous people, whom the Tory party wish to keep down and deprive of their rights, by com-pelling them to support the Established Church of England.

The gentlemen before us now, as belonging to the great Liberal party, repudiate that libel on the Established Church, and they see no cause why it should longer exist. All that we want is justice for Ireland, and we do not want it in any spirit of rivalry. It affects us little whether Roman Catholics, the Church of England, or the Dissenters are predominant; we simply say we are all fellow-men, and we recognise the great principle of doing unto others as we should wish to be done by. It is on this, therefore, that we join issue with our Tory opponents. We believe many of them to be sincere in their belief that an injury will be done to the Established Church. They think we are going to injure the State, but we say with all confidence, and perhaps no one here will hesitate to say with us, that we are as sure as we are of our existence that these predictions, like all the others they have started, will be falsified. Let me refer for one moment to the house of Devonshire, and the political questions now agitating this country. We see in the Duke of Devonshire a gentleman in every sense of the word, who has imbued his family with those lofty sympathies and feelings which ought to be the characteristics of citizens of this country. We find he has in Parliament three sons, and I have noted every vote they have given on any question of importance, and on every occasion every one of his sons has supported the popular cause thoroughly. I can also refer to the ancestors of the other candidate, and in doing so I speak particularly of the present Lord Belper. I don't know whether you remember as well as I do, but from the earliest time that I took an interest in politics I recollect the name of Edward Strutt as a man who stood forward to promote advancement in every direction. He then referred in terms of praise to the career of Lord Belper as a politician, and said he had always shown himself to be an earnest supporter of civil and religious liberty. He need scarcely refer to his perseverance as a commercial man, and although he was now a peer of the realm, he believed that he would prefer the name of Strutt to the title which had been conferred upon him in acknowledgment of the distinguished services he had rendered to his country. He hoped when his son, one of the candidates before them, succeeded to that title, he would have earned the laurels which adorn the brow of his father since he was promoted to the rank of peer. He then briefly introduced the candidates.

APPENDIX F.

Letters from Abroad.

HOTEL DE LOUVRE,
Nov. 13*th*, 1859.

You see we have actually run away from the old country, having left home on Friday morning, sleeping at Folkestone that night; crossing the Channel on Saturday, without any of the dreaded consequences of a sea-voyage, even to E——.

At Boulogne we enjoyed dinner, and rambled into the town and market-place, where we were amused and pleased with the assemblage of pleasant, cheerful-looking peasants, chiefly women, who, notwithstanding the number of English they must see, seemed to be amused with our amusement.

We reached Paris about eleven, and after a cursory examination of the luggage, which was "registered" for Paris, we were conveyed to the Hotel de Louvre, where they had attended to my instructions to provide rooms in the "higher part of the house, with a good aspect," as we are on the Quatrième Etage, looking over the Rue Rivoli and Rue de Marengo.

We have been walking and driving into the Bois de Boulogne, having a bright but cold day.

There was a good concourse of carriages and people. We were particularly pleased with the looks of the poorer class of women, with their neat white caps for their only head-dress, and with the soldiers, who, though short, have for the most part good countenances.

ROME, *Jan. 15th*, 1860.

We left Nice on the 27th December, after witnessing the finest storm we have ever seen. The Mediterranean was lashed into turbulence, and dashed furiously upon the rocky shores of Nice in masses of water and spray, greater in volume and height than we had seen on the west coast of Ireland or elsewhere. The ride from Nice to Genoa is magnificent, some portions of the route being in character and grandeur beyond imagining, and beyond my powers of description. It is almost entirely along the shores, that is, overlooking the Mediterranean, sometimes at an elevation of more than 2000 feet, sometimes on the sea-beach. The foliage has variety and richness even now, the oak and other trees not having entirely lost their foliage, the rich brown of which mingles with the dark green of the olive, and the light green of the orange, and the wilder-looking green of the stone pine.

VITTORIA HOTEL, NAPLES,
Jan. 28th, 1860.

MY DEAR A——,—Though we have not committed to paper all the good wishes of the season to you and your dear wife and bairns, we have often thought of you all in England, and indulged ourselves in conjectures as to your doings on Christmas Day and New Year's Day. The last is the first, and, I hope, only anniversary of these days we shall spend away from our own country and our own kith and kin.

It is true Christmas Day was spent among the English of Nice, with English fare for dinner; but this is not the same as having around one the merry faces of children and the sympathizing ones of old folks. You must not suppose that I mean to intimate that we were very gloomy in our comparative solitude, for that we were not, and you would think it strange if we repined that we could not have everything to make complete the enjoyment we are so lavishly indulging in.

As you have not heard of our proceedings, I think, since leaving Nice, I shall impose upon you a short narrative. We left Nice on the 28th December by vetturino, and slept at

Mentone, Oneglia, and Savona, arriving in Genoa on the 31st. This ride was indeed magnificent, unrivalled by anything we had seen before or have since seen, though that between Genoa and Pisa is almost as interesting, but is wanting in some of the most striking points of the first portion of the ride; and, coming upon you after instead of before the other, it does not excite the same bewilderment, I may say, of delight. Am I right in supposing that you know this route of the Riviera? If so, you will recollect the long ascent from Nice, commanding a most extensive view of the coast beyond Cannes, and embracing the chain of the Estrelles mountains; the town of Nice at your feet, with the deeply indented background of mountains, clothed with olive and orange trees, and pines, and evergreen oaks, with the sunny peaks in the distance; and then, after attaining the summit, the never-to-be-forgotten view of the depths of wooded slopes bounded by the Mediterranean.

Mentone seems to be becoming a favourite place of resort; we heard of it as being milder, more sheltered than either Cannes or Nice, and there seemed to be a good deal of building going on there. Looking at the inhabitants, we were rather unfavourably impressed, as many of the women looked sickly; but this might arise from their being over-worked, as we saw them carrying on their heads heavy loads of lemons, which they were bringing from the country into the town, and under which their frames seemed quite to riggle. It is possible, too, that they may be insufficiently fed, which would be quite sufficient in itself to account for any appearance of sickliness. The towns on this road are most of them quite peculiar with their very narrow streets, on entering which the vetturino would give a tremendous cracking of the whip, as if to warn all carts, mules, and bipeds to keep out of our way. Some of the larger of these towns have a most peculiar character. St. Remo, for instance, has an upper town, up which you climb as you would a ladder, with innumerable hand-ladders, your only guide to the top of the town being the rise of these ladders, and your only guide to your starting-point below being that through some one or more of these many stairs you are to descend to the base of the town. A town very like this we explored on a mountain road near Nice. It was on a mountain peak called Tourretti, which gave you the idea of being at the extreme confines of the earth, both in altitude and in every other respect, the half-civilised people flocking round us as though we were some extraordinary white people intruding into an aboriginal settlement.

After this little ethnological digression, let me take you back to the route between Nice and Genoa. After Mentone our next halting-place was Oneglia. . . . We reached Genoa without *contretemps*, of *mauvais temps*, or of any other description; remained there three days in bad weather; but otherwise should, no doubt, have been pleased with the surrounding country and with "La Superba" itself. We continued our journey by vetturino to Pisa,—a most interesting ride; stayed there three days, and then forward to Rome after visiting Leghorn; seeing, of course, the three, or I may say the quadrum, of interesting buildings assembled at Pisa. At Rome we only remained

two days, and posted on to Naples, across the Pontine
Marshes, and by Mola di Gaeta, a beautiful bay, much
smaller, but more picturesque than Naples,—at least this
is the impression at times; and then comes a bright sunny
day, when the headlands, the islands, Vesuvius, and the sea
are so lighted up that nothing which depends upon light
and shade for its effect can be more beautiful. How it
may be in the spring I do not know, but at this season we
miss the green fields and even leafless woods of England.

At Genoa and here we have had very many wet, gloomy
days, with howling raw wind. One of such days will be
followed frequently by one of the brightest sunshine, with a
light exhilarating air. Such was yesterday, when after service
at the French church we took a long walk into the country,
whilst to-day the wind is howling and the rain pouring
down from the lead-coloured clouds. Our sitting-room
looks upon the north-west side of the bay, but not on
Vesuvius. We had a fine day for those most interesting
ruins of Pompeii, which were more extensive, perfect, and
interesting than we had anticipated. We ascended
Vesuvius on a very fine day. E—— and I rode to the foot
of the cone, which E—— mounted with no other aid than a
stick. There is a slight eruption going on from a lower
point of the mountain below the base of the cone.

Rome, *Feb. 26th*, 1860.

I confess that I was rather disappointed with Naples and
its bay. This is so frequently the case when you have
heard a place extolled very highly. The imagination

begins to invest it with all your ideal of beauty, and if
it fails to come up to this, even in any respect, there is
a feeling of disappointment. On some of the few fine
days we had there, the general disposition of the coast, the
headlands, and more especially of the islands fringing and
set in the sea, appeared very picturesque and interesting, but
the absence of fine trees and of green swelling meadows and
wooded ravines prevents its realizing all that goes to make
up a perfectly beautiful coast. We did not see the bay
from the sea, the weather being uninviting for nautical
expeditions, and thus we did not see, as part of the Bay of
Naples, some portions of its wide expanse which are very
beautiful, but which we saw from the land rather as so
many distinct bays.

On some sunny days especially our admiration of the
whole was indeed almost unbounded, and it seems unfair
to saddle it with the impressions which had their birth on
dull days, when the hypercritical and dissatisfied spirit was
in the ascendant.

Having taken the more westerly route from Rome to
Naples, we returned to Rome by the more easterly route,
by Capua (common to the two routes), San Germano, and
Ferrentino, travelling by vetturino, and occupying three
days. The country is interesting, and the peasantry, the
women I mean, prettier looking and more picturesquely
dressed than any we had seen in Italy.

On arriving at San Germano we found the place filled
with Neapolitan soldiers. They had no room at the first
inn we applied at, and at the other they had officers

quartered in the house, but we had no annoyance from them; on the contrary, they were very civil and obligingly disposed in smoothing away little difficulties that presented themselves.

We set off at five in the morning after our arrival at San Germano to see the celebrated monastery of Monte Casino, reputed the finest in the world. The church is remarkably rich in marble and wood‑carving. The situation of the monastery is very fine, being perched on a peak some 2000 feet high. Our ascent was lighted by the moon, which shone forth from under the lowering clouds as we wound up the mountain, E—— on a donkey, the rest on foot. The morning did not become fine enough to make the view from the summit as extensive or interesting as it would otherwise have been. The abbot kindly came to us in the library, which is rich in literary curiosities. When I say " us," I mean R—— and myself; for womenkind are not admissible except to the church, where E—— and M—— had ample time to remain and admire.

ROME, *Feb. 26th,* 1860.

The statuary in the Museum of the Capitol is very interesting. "The Dying Gladiator" and the " Venus of the Capitol" are very fine. The latter would, I think, be perfect if the face was beautiful, which, according to my taste, it is not. It is a good face, no doubt, according to rule, but there is an absence of the sweetness which is essential to beauty or loveliness. "The Dying Gladiator" strikes me as perfect. The figure most admirably formed, and the face and expression of the limbs telling the history of the vanquished and mortally wounded man. There are some very spirited bas-reliefs, and a great many interesting busts, etc.

VIENNA, *June 8th,* 1873.

Yesterday I ran off to see the Semmering, there being no hope of Russell's joining me. It is very interesting and extraordinary — the railway meandering amongst the mountains in a wonderful manner—now crossing a gorge, suddenly through a tunnel at the end of which you look down into the deep gorge below, with pinnacles of wooded rock rising from the depths; some of these rock pinnacles rising above your head—on some you look down. In some cases you pass a place, and after travelling six or eight miles find yourself within a mile or so of the same place, but at a great height above it. The great charm of the Semmering is the magnificent aggregation of the wooded rock, peaks, and gorges, near the summit. I left at 7 A.M. and got back (to Vienna) about 10 P.M., having gone as far as Gratz on the route to Trieste.

APPENDIX G.

The Funeral Ceremony.

From the " Derbyshire Courier," Nov. 28, 1885.

On Saturday afternoon the interment of Mr. Frederick Swanwick, J.P., of Whittington House, near Chesterfield, took place at the Chesterfield Cemetery. The large and representative gathering which attended the funeral on Saturday was a testimony to the esteem and respect in which Mr. Swanwick was held by all classes in the town and neighbourhood. Amongst the gentlemen present were members of the committees of the Chesterfield and North Derbyshire Hospital, the Institute of Engineers, the Art School, the Mechanics' Institute, the Science School, and the University Extension movement, with all of which Mr. Swanwick had been connected, and the assemblage included a considerable number of personal friends.

The funeral service was conducted by the Rev. J. F. Smith, of Mansfield, formerly minister of the Elder Yard Chapel at Chesterfield. At the conclusion of the service in the chapel, the following address was delivered : —" Fellow-mourners, this solemn occasion is one which both our grief and our gratitude command us not to let pass without some special reference to the loss which this neighbourhood, and a still wider circle, has sustained by the death of our brother whose mortal remains we are about to commit to the kind bosom of the earth which he loved and brightened by his presence. Our departed friend was one of her brightest, purest, and kindest sons, and his removal leaves a void which cannot be filled up, not only in his home and circle of personal acquaintances, but in this district generally. A public man of a noble type, and of a marked character, whose career was notable and influence beneficent, has passed away from us. His death is not only an irreparable loss to his family and personal friends, it is a public loss and a public sorrow. Nor is it only a small circle of intimate acquaintances who are called upon to-day thankfully to mark his virtues and his deeds; throughout this district and beyond it he was known and loved as a *man* and as a constant and munificent friend of all movements for the enlightenment and elevation of his fellow-men. Yet while large numbers had learned to respect and revere the strength, the purity, and the benevolence of his character, or to rely upon his steady advocacy and liberal support of every good cause which commended itself to his independent judgment, it was those who knew him best, and who had known him longest, who perceived how strong and good he was; it was they who knew him as one of those absolutely true men who never fail their friends or cause—as one of those pure, unselfish souls who never know when they have done enough for others, and never think of themselves—as one of those bright spirits who make it their mission, whatever their own sorrow may be, to carry light and gladness into the hearts and lives of others, whether young or old—as one of those sympathetic, painstaking, and cautious advisers who make the interests of others their own,—it was only those who knew him personally in some of these illustrations of his strength and goodness who could form any remote idea how great that strength and goodness were. As he passes from us, therefore, he leaves behind him the great record that to know him most was most to revere and love him. But while his finer qualities were revealed in the trying light of long and close intimacy, which surely created absolute trust and unbounded regard, his qualities as a public man could be known and read of all men. His power of mastering a matter to its minutest details, the conscientious thoroughness with which he executed every task he undertook, were amongst the qualities which not only secured for him his eminent position in his profession, but also gave to his work the enduring character of which it can boast, the benefit of which the world reaps to-day, and will reap for years to come. The same characteristics, enriched by the noble qualities of his heart, reappeared in the latter portion of his life, when, in freedom from professional labour, he devoted himself entirely to public duties. As a magistrate, he conscientiously 'sought out the cause that he knew not,' was prone to take the side of the weak against the strong, and ever loved to temper justice with mercy. One of the noblest institutions of the county—the Chesterfield Hospital—was indebted in a great degree to his deep and constant interest, his large liberality, and his business sagacity. As it was to the spread of education, and of education as adapted to the wants of the present age, that he looked more particularly for lessening human misery and effecting the elevation of our race, his philanthropy showed itself prominently in the promotion of education. It is not elementary education alone that loses in him a devoted friend; every movement and institution of the neighbourhood designed to promote liberal culture suffers immeasurably by his removal. His devotion to the work of education was, however, but the predominant form which his fine and deep philanthropy assumed. He loved and believed in his fellow-men, and looked forward with a religious fervour too deep for words to the better time coming for one and all. This faith and hope made him a true reformer and warm advocate and promoter of human progress in every form that his judgment could approve. He thus became a staunch friend and ally of large numbers of brave and self-denying labourers in God's vineyard, some of whom, like himself, have been called away from this scene of their devoted toil, while others mourn with us to-day that his voice is silent and his hand still. But he being dead yet speaketh in the higher tones of the spirit, and by the noble example of his life bids us show our love for him by loving more purely the divine things for which he delighted to labour, and in which he found his deepest joy. His spirit and his life likewise bid those who to-day mourn the loss in him of a personal friend not to yield to the paralysis of sorrow. Those who love him most feel most the light of his character and his life—a light undying and full of cheerful hope and blessed immortality."

MORRISON AND GIBB, EDINBURGH,
PRINTERS TO HER MAJESTY'S STATIONERY OFFICE.

www.ingramcontent.com/pod-product-compliance
Lightning Source LLC
Chambersburg PA
CBHW020759020726
47495CB00008B/2513